IN THE TIME OF THE GIRLS

In the Time of the Girls

By Anne Germanacos

American Reader Series, No. 14

BOA Editions, Ltd. ～ Rochester, NY ～ 2010

First Edition
09 10 11 12 7 6 5 4 3 2 1

For information about permission to reuse any material from this book please contact The Permissions Company at www.permissionscompany.com or e-mail permdude@eclipse.net.

Publications by BOA Editions, Ltd. – a not-for-profit corporation under section 501 (c) (3) of the United States Internal Revenue Code – are made possible with funds from a variety of sources, including public funds from the New York State Council on the Arts, a state agency; the Literature Program of the National Endowment for the Arts; the County of Monroe, NY; the Lannan Foundation for support of the Lannan Translations Selection Series; the Sonia Raiziss Giop Charitable Foundation; the Mary S. Mulligan Charitable Trust; the Rochester Area Community Foundation; the Arts & Cultural Council for Greater Rochester; the Steeple-Jack Fund; the Ames-Amzalak Memorial Trust in memory of Henry Ames, Semon Amzalak and Dan Amzalak; and contributions from many individuals nationwide.

See Colophon on page 180 for special individual acknowledgements.

Cover Design: Sandy Knight
Cover Art: Belinda Bryce
Interior Design and Composition: Bill Jones
Manufacturing: Thomson-Shore
BOA Logo: Mirko

Library of Congress Cataloging-in-Publication Data
Germanacos, Anne.
In the time of the girls : stories / by Anne Germanacos. -- 1st ed.
   p. cm.
ISBN 978-1-934414-38-5 (alk. paper)
I. Title.
PS3607.E77I53 2010
811'.6--dc22

2010009196

BOA Editions, Ltd.
250 North Goodman Street, Suite 306
Rochester, NY 14607
www.boaeditions.org
A. Poulin, Jr., Founder (1938-1996)

NATIONAL
ENDOWMENT
FOR THE ARTS
A great nation
deserves great art.

State of the Arts

NYSCA

For Nick

Table of Contents

In the Time of the Girls	9
Boundaries	19
Ovid Sings	26
Until We Go to Sleep	34
Men on Crosses	42
Infinity	51
Eros	57
Being Black	62
Anthropology	68
Her Dowry	74
Mary	80
Killing the Husband	88
All the Men	93
Adam and Eva	101
Grace	107
His Mother's Cats	119
Sundering Twins	128
Courting Monsters	135
Ginka's Perfume	139
Twenty-nine Stones for You to Hold	143
Caffeine	154
Being Conquered	162
Twirling Dervishes	170
Acknowledgments	176
About the Author	177
Colophon	180

In the Time of the Girls

Death of the Time

I'm not sure what I think or know anymore, now, in the days of the departed girls. You could even call it the death of the time of the girls.

Those girls are still too real. If I don't forget about them and let them flow out to sea, the tide will never bring them back.

Flies, Dead Kitten

A month after their departure, flies swarm. The peacock's moan is obnoxious and insistent.

Walking, I pass a dead kitten. The placenta is there, flies hover. When I go back later, the kitten is gone.

But where?

The mother came and pulled it away, though it was dead? A hawk flew down and swooped it up?

(Things come and go.)

The Girls:

Hera's sudden pains. Her angers and hilarities, her fluctuations. Her very long blond-streaked hair. The eyes that, once almost too clear, are now opaque. Her crazy mother, the only (other) family she has.

Artemis' elaborate dreams, her money, her jewelry, her clothes (blue sunglasses), her drawings that are more doodle than anything recognizable. Her family like a piece of complicated architecture.

Demeter's hair in ponytails, her funny teeth. Her mature beauty when she smiles. The mother she loves to hate. Her boa, rat, pygmy goats.

Athena's rage to make words say things she doesn't yet know. Her lack of experience. Her weenie of a father. The mother she says is like a father.

The junk food Hera buys for them.
Artemis' soy milk.
Demeter's vegetarianism. (Her mother's lesbianism.)

Athena's worry that she'll become like her Italian grandmother whose bra has made grooves in her shoulders from being weighed down with breasts.

STAR

They used to say my name frequently, as if it gave them joy or a thrill to do so. I rarely said their names. Like a star, I just made my entrance or exit with a general hello or goodbye.

ONE

The way they pushed all the boundaries, wanting to be part of the same thing. Wanting, in essence, to be not many but one.

NIRVANA ICE CREAM

The day Demeter found the new mother cat and four kittens, the rest of the girls and I ate Nirvana brand ice cream as we watched her nuzzle and kiss them. Nirvana, another order of religion entirely, has nothing to do with Greek goddesses.

Still, they shoveled it in.

GENIUS

The day I handed back Athena's story, the one on which I had written

NEVER USE THESE WORDS AGAIN: soul, mysterious, perfection

She said: "You were so angry when you wrote this."
I said: "No, I was just being adamant."
She said: "But they're the words I use, the most important words."
I said: "Ditch them."
She said: "Thanks."

She always thanked me for being tough—criticism didn't faze her.

A week or so later, she wrote a paragraph about the things we do to our bodies, using words like shave, feed, touch, ending with something about a little pile of charred, blackened bones.

That was pure genius.

BREASTFEEDING BABY TIGERS

Once, in class, they stopped me in the middle and told me about an Indonesian woman who breastfed baby tigers!

PINK UGGS

We tried on the boots, kicked them off. Got excited, scared, felt them taking off, soared.

Those shoes were our rocket-pad, our launch to the sun where we mingled for nanoseconds with the rays, delighting in the exquisite burn.

With the boots on our feet, the girls turned older, I regained youth. Years added and subtracted so quickly that our ages mingled and signified nothing but the fact of our being on the earth.

We danced a vigorous conversation in those pink boots.

STARBUCKS

Missing frappucinos, they made themselves sick on thin squares of dark chocolate dipped in the endless cups of Illy espresso I supplied them with.

SMOKING

After class, they trash-talked in the courtyard.

Each girl told how long she'd been smoking, how many times she'd already quit, who she'd lied to about smoking or quitting, how many cigarettes she'd smoked that day.

Hera was in a horrible mood, pulling on a hand-rolled cigarette as if it were a joint.

I said "Stop smoking that cigarette as if it's a joint" and everyone laughed.

IMPROVISATION

What did we talk about? Mostly nothing. It was a style of communication, more tone than content.

The flim-flam of everything said, now lost.

SHARING

We took turns with the boots. They turned sad or nervous energy into a dance. Someone was always having a nervous breakdown, or about to. Things were understood without being stated.

We talked a cool dance, knit shapes with our words.

FRESH-FACED

My fresh-faced girls, each with a fixation or two.

In the Time of the Girls

ABSTRACT

Girls. The kind of things girls do. The kinds of girl on this earth. The things they wear, and what they eat (or don't eat). What they think sex will be (and what it ends up being, for girls, still not women). What girls do to boys. Girls riding horses. Girls cutting their hair or keeping it long, getting gum stuck in it, high up near the scalp. Wearing boots, sandals, flip-flops (mostly flip-flops). Barefoot girls stepping on glass, pulling glass from an instep, watching the blood drip onto dry dirt. Smiling. Unhorrified. Or, horrified, screaming.

Girls playing in cardboard houses their fathers put together while they slept. Girls running outside to find their cardboard houses flattened by the night's rain.

Girls with scars in difficult-to-find places.

Girls eating dirt.
Paper napkins, candle wax. Girls throwing up.

Girls in the middle of natural disasters: aborting fetuses, cutting hair, slashing wrists. Fording rivers.

Girls without brothers.
Girls menstruating.
Girls condemned by menstruation.

Girls stolen by Indian chiefs.
Menstruating girls swimming in the ocean, attacked by sharks.

IN CLASS

The girls shifted in their seats, waiting for me to continue.

I wondered: Are they really listening? And even if they think they are, what's the precise quality of their attention?

Girls drift and dream. I know. I, too, was once a girl.

MORE GIRLS

Girls crying, girls screaming, girls wearing short skirts and high pink boots. Girls painting their nails blue, their lips silver, increasing the darkness of their eyelashes. Girls calling out in pain (some of it psychic). Girls hating each other, girls making alliances, girls destroying each other and girls making up.

Girls eating buttered toast.

Girls making boys jealous.
Girls singing.

Girls without siblings. Girls with too many brothers.
Adopted girls. (Aborted girls? Pinpricks of being floating out to sea?)
Overmedicated girls.

Unreadable girls.
Insinuating girls.

The luck of boys.
The insult of girls.

Fatherless girls.
Girls with hovering mothers.

Girls with clothes strewn everywhere.

Naked girls.
Tattooed girls.
Hairy girls.
Squeaky clean girls.

Girls feeding boas.
Girls birthing babies.
Giving blow jobs.

Girls crying out in pleasure.
Girls listening to other girls, in neighboring beds.

Whispering girls. Girls running like the wind. Cantering horsey girls!

ROULA, A WOMAN

One night I dreamt that Roula, the cook and our friend, was at a doctor's appointment. When she came out of the office, she was crying. We all knew it was because she had cancer. The doctor wanted to get in right away and see if it had spread to the bone.

Blissful girls.
Ill girls.

Radiant girls.
Hungry girls. Willful girls.

Wannabe girls.

Fat girls.
Sloppy girls.

Incredulous girls.
Compromised girls.
Immaculate girls.

GINKA, ANOTHER WOMAN

Ginka, a woman from Bulgaria, takes care of a childless old woman who pees everywhere, though she shits at the base of a tree.

Every time Ginka arrives to clean her up, she finds a filthy key around the woman's neck. The woman won't let Ginka touch the key, so it filthies all her nightgowns at that spot.

I understand Ginka's frustration at not being able to make the old woman immaculate the way she would a child or her own mother.

MORE GIRLS IN ACTION

Uncompromising girls.

Plaid girls.
Scotchguard girls.
Intimate apparel girls.

Wigged-out girls.
Girl junkies.

Pharmaceutical girls.
Brand-name girls.

Vicious girls.
Ancient girls.

Glorious girls.

Lactating girls.
Ovulating girls.

Starving girls.
Amazon girls.
Olympiad girls!

Once

My mother was once a girl.

And I, writing of girls, am a girl no longer.

Girls

Girls and their vanity!
Their insecurity!
Their omnivorousness!

Girls eating everything, leaving nothing.
Starving girls, wizened girls.

Infantile girls.
Athletic girls.

Girls pleasuring boys pleasuring girls.
Moony girls.

Hearkening girls.

Vain girls. Phantom girls. Illicit girls. Sinning girls. Creeping girls. Scathing girls. Girls travelling. Girls talking. Across the ages.

EUTHANASIA

One spring afternoon, Athena promised to kill me if someday my brain stops functioning but I'm still alive.

SMUGGLING

I smuggled small gifts to them: squares of blue-paper-wrapped chocolate. Mugs of steaming coffee. The forgotten words to songs. Cotton socks when theirs got wet in the rain. Ice for sprains and bruises. Hearty soups with thick crusty bread.

No snakes, nothing made of fish, no insects.

MORE

Relentless girls. Mimicking girls.
Imitation girls?
Pure girls.

Barbaric girls. Angelic girls. Postulant girls.

Disastrous girls. Banished girls.
Desultory girls. Fractious girls.
Nonchalant girls.
Womanly girls.

Disaffected girls. Manic girls.

REBECCA SOLNIT

Says that, as a girl, she always felt she would die young.

In her book, *A Field Guide to Getting Lost,* she says: "…teenagers imagine dying young because death is more imaginable than the person that all the decisions and burdens of adulthood may make of you."

Dream girls, as in all the songs.

Factotum girls.

Heartless girls.
Feckless girls.

Ecstatic girls. Forlorn girls.

Homesick girls. Nostalgic girls.

Girls in attitudes of prayer.
Girls holding their arms to the wind.
Girls hastening.

Girls singing gospel.
Girls

In their company, I could lose myself over and over again, a veritable tumult of lost and found.

BOUNDARIES

Mornings, they're the first people she sees: the clown woman or Nathan, outside Revery, warming their hands on large paper cups of coffee. She exchanges a nod with them, orders her own.

Back home, awakening her son for school, Elizabeth sits at the foot of his bed, tells him it's time. Jonah groans, half-asleep, and pushes her off the bed. Neither of them wants her to be there when he emerges, naked, from the sheets. In six months, he'll be leaving for college. In the meantime, they're negotiating the territory.

THE BAKERY

Weekdays in the neighborhood, a homeless man sits at the communal table at the bakery for hours. He's always hooked up to at least three different machines: part of a transistor radio, a piece of computer, and something else, unidentifiable. His hair's never combed; his shoes are split along the sides.

This place serves the best French roast and he knows it. Or maybe, Elizabeth thinks as she buys a loaf of bread, it's just the easiest place for him to navigate with all that gear attached. He provides his own answer to the people who sit and stare at computer screens. In there, everyone's hooked up.

One Sunday night, a neighbor's dog discovers stacks of old bread, piles of broken pastry shells, leftover tarte tatin outside the bakery on the street. Elizabeth arranges with the owner to give the old food to the homeless shelter, agrees to pick it up each night just before closing time.

Public Shower

The homeless people shower on the sidewalk, using the green-and-black hoses hooked up to the houses. Sometimes, by mistake, they leave their free-sample bottles of Prell on Elizabeth's steps. Her son Jonah grabs a bottle, brings it inside. She makes him take it out again, leave it where he found it. "It's not yours," she says.

She sees him wondering if his mother's all right in her mind. In a few months, he'll be leaving. Is he worried about himself, or about her? And who's *she* more worried about, a bottle of Prell coming between them?

Outside Revery

Nathan wakes up coughing, spitting. It happens all night long; mornings, Elizabeth sees a puddle of dense, clotted saliva near the doorway of the café. Chub, the dog, sleeps on Nathan's matted hair, holding it tight to the sidewalk.

She watches a tiny cherubic child, green eyes bright, go close on rubber soles. The child treads on Nathan, climbs with clutching hands as if the man's a spongy mountain. Hands reach matted hair when Nathan coughs deeply. Someone spills hot coffee on them both. The child wails. Nathan sits up, checks the sores on his blackened feet.

Elizabeth seems to see him thinking: What I could do with a dog *and* a baby. Coins would drip from well-wishers' hands.

Four Minutes

The homeless people had four minutes, they were told, to decide which things they'd keep. A dump truck idled, double-parked, behind the police car.

Sinbad kept his blanket and a sackful of Monopoly money. The clown woman added several layers of clothing to what she was already wearing. Arthur, Cleopatra, and Lily weren't around; Ramona looked like she was trying to guess what they'd want, but the whole thing happened so quickly it was probably impossible for her to think about what *she* wanted to keep, let alone what someone else desired. Her hands hung down; she looked dismayed.

When the truck pulled away, everyone on the street, including the ones behind the windows, felt pervaded by helplessness. Eventually the homeless people walked away, as if they had someplace to go.

FREE

When Jonah outgrew his shoes, Converse, Nikes or New Balance, Elizabeth put them on the sidewalk a little to the right of the stairway leading up to their house. Generally, the shoes were gone within a few hours.

Once, months later, she discovered that he'd taken them back inside on his way home from school. After that, she put the shoes out at night so they'd be taken while he slept. His closet was overflowing. She had no idea how he'd decide what to take, what to leave behind.

MONKEY HAIR

One of the homeless people has straight black hair out of which rises something light brown, teased and full, angling over like a top-heavy ice cream cone but alive-seeming too. At first Elizabeth thought it was a monkey but finally she got close enough to see that it was just more, but different, hair.

As he passes her house, he laughs hysterically, drunkenly. Then he crosses over to the park and sits on the grass. Sometimes, he lunges out at her as she goes by. Most days she tries to make herself invisible, keeping her eyes away from him, her feet walking a respectful distance. Occasionally, something in her rises to the challenge of him. She pauses, looks at him. Before continuing, she smiles.

4TH OF JULY

The summer before, several of the neighbors roasted a whole sheep on the sidewalk in front of their houses, then invited passersby to come over and sample the barbecue.

They met people they'd never spoken to, including some of the homeless people, who came by one at a time, as if they were afraid to frighten the people who lived in houses. Up close, Elizabeth saw how each person's skin had been painfully burnt by the sun and wanted to hand them sunscreen, as she would Jonah.

With a beer in one hand and a rib in the other, Elizabeth noticed that she and the clown woman were wearing the exact same shoes. New Balance 803s. Elizabeth's were tan, the clown woman's were navy.

The clown woman moves through the neighborhood wrapped in layers of colorful clothing, like a large, loosely-swaddled baby. As she walks, the bells attached to her ankles and hanging from her neck jangle.

Cone-shaped hat on her head, the clown woman had taken out her tarot cards and set them up on a step leading to Elizabeth's house. When she went near, the clown woman gathered the deck in her hands, as if to begin the reading. But Elizabeth just wanted to talk. With a couple of beers inside, it was easy for her to blurt: "You know, we've got the exact same shoes." The clown woman's sun-burnt eyelids came down over her harsh blue eyes—she seemed to smile.

The meat, cooked on a makeshift barbecue, was impossibly tough. The next morning, they found globs of chewed meat strewn along the street, mostly in the gutters and at the foot of various trees.

SIGN ON A TELEPHONE POLE:

Looking for a child, preferably a baby

Elizabeth is stunned, wonders who would post such a message. Is it a joke?

STOLEN GOODS

Just before seven at night, Elizabeth arrives in her station wagon, parks on the curb, opens the trunk.

In the evenings lit by the bakery's all-season red-and-green Christmas lights, she piles day-old pastries and bread into the car for the night. Mornings, the man from the homeless shelter collects everything: tarts, napoleons, chocolate mousse. Baguettes.

She's always known it would happen: they use baseball bats on the car windows and run off with everything. Tarte tatin and strawberry tarts. She doesn't know if she's fooling herself or just hopeful, insisting to Jonah that they must have been very hungry.

COPS

It's December, the air is cold. She watches the cops circle their beat, wondering what they feel, shining flashlights against closed eyes. Do they sometimes resist duty and let the homeless people sleep spread out beneath the bushes, heads under cardboard? Like gods, do they give and withhold sleep?

FORTUNATE WEATHER

That day was unseasonably clear.

The next-door neighbors had put up signs on telephone poles in the neighborhood, lime-green paper with bold black print: GARAGE SALE, EVERYTHING GOES.

Apparently, the husband and wife weren't looking for anything in particular. It was just a good day for them to be out with the baby. The sun was shining, and while there was a breeze, it wasn't enough to blow off the red hat that made the little girl look like a small Mother Hubbard.

They said afterwards that the mother of the baby thought the baby's father was holding her; the father was certain he'd handed the baby to her mother. Someone remembered the mother was leafing through old comic books. The father was seen holding a broken fishing pole.

It was a cool, blue-skied day. A mild breeze picked up very light objects and let them down again, a little skewed. When the breeze stiffened slightly, the baby was discovered missing. By then it was just past noon.

The homeless people were down at the shelter, biting into croissants and tarts.

While the neighborhood searched along the sidewalks and in alleyways, up stairs and inside houses, the baby was eating almond paste pressed to her lips on fat childish fingers.

Later, the fat child, a boy, said the baby made an "O" mouth for him, said the baby's cheeks moved as if it were drinking the almonds. Even then, he couldn't take his hands off the baby, who lolled happily in her mother's arms.

THINGS

When Elizabeth leaves things, it's at night. She puts sunscreen, almonds, and books on the street beneath the magnolia tree outside her house. She knows she should just walk into the park and hand it all to the clown woman or one of the others, but she's terrified. What if they don't want any of it? What else does she have to give?

Jonah sees the bundles on the street when he leaves for school in the morning. Knowing they're hers, he says, "Mom, what about your jewelry? Why don't you give away those dangly earrings you like so much? What about those plates of Grandma's? I'm sure they'd like those."

The day he finishes packing up the things he'll take with him when he goes, they're barely speaking. She knows it's something that happens, to make the separation easier. She also knows that she'll cry as soon as he turns and walks toward the plane.

She goes out to get him a deli sandwich for the trip. On the way back, she passes the park, sees the clown woman there alone on a green bench, blowing on the open mouth of a paper cup. The woman raises her head to show Elizabeth that she's seen her.

The clown woman's blue gaze seems amused in a dreamy way, and while Elizabeth wonders if she's on drugs or if it's just the way her eyes contrast with such sunburnt skin, she hears her say, "The woman with my shoes! Just the one I've been waiting for."

Elizabeth walks close, stands near. Each woman's feet, clad in 803s, are a mirror of the other's. Sadness makes her bold. "Are those really all the clothes you own?"

"These are what I've got today—but I'm always adding, subtracting."

Elizabeth wants desperately to tell her there's going to be an extra room in her house, but just thinking it brings tears. Leaning forward on the bench, the clown woman takes her hand, looks at the lines, and offers her a whole new life.

Ovid Sings

Changed Bodies

Ovid sings of bodies changed.

It may have happened when, six years ago, Olivia was visiting us on the island and lightning struck the house. We smelled burnt hair and were terrified that the lightning might have danced through her body. But there were no other indications, so this must have been our imagination—mine and her father's. Still, we liked to tell people it had happened.

It's more likely the change in her occurred when none of us were looking—least of all she herself, Olivia.

Acceptable Names

The cat has a variety of names. Olivia's daughter Eleni made them up as she went along, first using words that rhymed with Fluffy, the one he answered to—Muffy, Puffy, Stuffy; then going farther afield—Frosty, Chimpanzee, Cleopatra. The latter, an odd name for a male, is acceptable in that household where men are, for the most part, banned.

I tried calling him Fred, but the cat ignored me; Eleni began to smile, but turned it into a wounded frown.

ELENI AND OLGA

One morning Eleni found her Barbie dolls tumbled, legs scissored between legs, arms in the air. By that afternoon, she and her friend Olga were in her bed together, with a Ken doll between them. In a harsh embrace, breathing hard, eight years old, Eleni coughed into Olga's ear; Olga coughed back. Olga looked like a girl, but then she looked like a boy.

The Barbies had started it—the way they'd rearranged their limbs in the night, offering themselves to her like a bright idea. She remembered later that there hadn't been anything so tender as a kiss.

So where had it begun? At the root of her body, behind the belly button, which connected to that button between her legs. Once, in a fit of generosity, she'd shown her father the precise location. He'd turned away, embarrassed. "Those are women's things," he'd said. Eleni knew then that her father would never ever turn girl.

STRUCK

If it did happen that way, what was the feel of the *sizzle* when the electricity went through Olivia? We were sure we could smell her hair, wiry to begin with, then further frazzled by the invisible heat.

She'd been reading *Like Water for Chocolate*, almost salivating over its descriptions of food and love, when lightning struck the house. Should we have run to her, grabbed her hands with our own, letting electricity course through us as well? Would that have protected her from the instantaneous change of body, love, and fate?

DRINKING WITH OLIVIA

I'd known what Olivia was going to tell me, the day she'd called and asked me to fly in for a quick visit. She had to talk to me, she'd said.

"Okay, you're gay," I'd practiced in my imagination. "So what was the important thing you were going to tell me?" By then it was obvious, no big deal. By then, even her father and I spoke of it almost casually.

Olivia and I sipped our most recent favorite adult drink, scotch. Ever since I'd married her father, periods in our life together were marked by the beverage we'd favored: Batida de Coco, Tia Maria, and so on.

After she offered her revelation, I told her about practicing for our conversation. We laughed together, then clinked glasses in perfect-seeming understanding.

"It turns out I'm a breast woman!" Olivia said. I thought of her father, who likes every part of a woman's body, and simply smiled.

Think Cinderella or Snow White: we weren't supposed to love one another, yet we did, we do.

PUZZLE

When Eleni grew frustrated, bored, or confused, she would empty a box of puzzle pieces onto the low coffee table in Olivia's living room. She had piles of those boxes in her room, stacked under her bed, on the shelves, in her closet. She liked the one with five-hundred pieces (Hercules, the Flintstones, the Little Mermaid) but sometimes had to settle for two hundred, or even one hundred and fifty. Sometimes her mother would say, "Five more minutes," and Eleni would race the clock.

Rather than leaving a puzzle unfinished, she'd slide it off the table onto the floor. Gazing down at the shattered puzzle, she knew the foolishness of trying to make many things into one, knew instead that one thing was so often more things than it seemed.

RIDDLE

In a house of two women and one girl, does the girl have two mothers? Or two who are *like* mothers?

Sometimes, when Olivia and Sappho are yelling at life's injustices, Eleni tells them her joke about the dumb woman who thought corn flakes were a puzzle and sat around all morning trying to put the flakes together into a likeness of the rooster on the front of the cereal box. When she tells the joke, when all three of them smile at it, isn't Eleni being like a mother herself?

Mothering: never less than a two-way street, and more often than not, a genuine puzzle.

EMPATHY

After I told my husband Olivia's news, he was adamant that his mother, Olivia's grandmother, shouldn't be told. She was eighty-two, her husband was gone, pain in one of her legs kept her up at night, she couldn't hear the high notes in Beethoven's symphonies any longer.

He wanted her to be spared that particular bit of information about her favorite granddaughter. I promised not to tell, though I was sure the revelation would be less disconcerting to her than he seemed to think. I *wanted* to tell her; I thought she deserved to know.

My husband insists that Olivia's business is her own. But who has time for lies?

COSTUMES

Eleni used to have four costumes. The skirt of the first, a gypsy costume, was so wide it circled almost as high as her face when she went round. The second costume was that of Ariel, the mermaid: turquoise blue, with something into which she zipped both feet. (How did she move in that one?) Then there was Cinderella, who limped around in one shoe.

The fourth was the one she wore as she relayed to me the whole history of her costume-wear. Standing before me, she was Cleopatra. The night before, we'd watched part of the film. Now she twirled around, jumped onto furniture, walked the back of the sofa along the wall, jumped down to the marble floor—like a sister to her cat, Fluffy, now a boy dressed only in hairy grey.

When he jumped onto my lap, she said: "He doesn't need a costume!" She scooped him away and held him in her arms like a baby, nudging his belly with her forehead, unconcerned that I might've liked to hold him for a while longer.

The cat's warm body, clothed in simple grey fur, was a magnet for our hands.

KUNG FU

Sporting a new boyish haircut, Eleni sliced the air with Kung Fu hands. In the basement room many children in black outfits with white tigers emblazoned across their backs, cut the air with quick, violent moves. Both of Eleni's mothers were watching from the sidelines. Olivia looked rapturous; Sappho's arms were crossed in a gesture of defensiveness.

Heron, tiger, snake. There was a scent of stale young sweat. Throughout, Eleni kept a furious look on her face to hide the happiness she felt mimicking dragon, eagle, and her favorite, panther.

At home, she refused to undress. Eventually the apartment was pervaded with the smell of all the animals she'd been, including snake.

CAUTION

Olivia's scalp showed through her fine curly hair. Once it had been a siren song, its long curls swaying with the wind as if they were water. Now her hair had changed.

Olivia told me that one night, gripped by jealousy, Sappho had wanted to burn off that mass. She'd held a cigarette near. Nothing had happened, though, and the next day Sappho had found the lump—not in her own breast but Olivia's, as she'd held her from behind.

I noticed that Sappho was always very careful with her cigarettes.

MERRY-GO-ROUND

I fantasize that Olivia dies and Eleni is left to me. I give her better presents on her birthday, brighter balloons, thicker frosting. The fantasy picks up speed, like a merry-go-round, and I imagine the books I'll read to her, the lessons she'll have—jazz piano and Italian, water ballet, and painting—until the reality of what I'm doing sinks in.

In the future, I jump off quickly, as soon as the fantasy starts to whirl.

BREASTS

One day, in the bathtub, Eleni noticed that her breasts were swelling.

Her mother's breast, the right one, had a long scar that started in the thickness and ran until it stopped in the pit of her underarm. Eleni wondered what her father would say about the long red scar. It reminded her of thin, twisted rope.

Not wanting diseases, she refrained from touching the cat. Until then, Stuffy had been her best friend, the only male allowed in the house. Now Eleni shooed him away whenever he jumped onto her lap, and washed her hands even when she brushed against him by mistake.

She didn't want to go without breasts.

As she got out of the tub, Stuffy sidled close, rubbed against her wet leg. Eleni kicked hard, sent him flying. Then, without a word, she jumped back into the tub and kicked at the water until the bathroom was soaked.

Stepping gingerly to avoid slipping, Olivia entered and handed Eleni the phone—it was her father—then left, closing the bathroom door behind her.

When she told me, I wondered if Olivia ever missed Eleni's father, but didn't dare ask.

Nearly Crying

Olivia called me on the verge of crying, said she'd been thinking of me. Wouldn't I come and visit her? "Of course," I said. "Do you want me to get on the afternoon plane?" "No, next weekend," she said. "I'll be feeling well enough then. Now I can't even get up the stairs."

If she were taken away from us, her father would be devastated, her daughter would be maimed. But what about me? We'd grown up together, nearly sisters, sometimes playing mother or daughter to each other, always friends. How many different losses is that?

Wooden Leg

"I'm not sure I should be the one who tells you this, but I think you ought to know."

It wasn't, perhaps, the best way to begin the conversation with my mother-in-law. Once I'd started, though, I couldn't go back.

She was resting her bad leg on a footstool between us. It pained her, she said, especially in the night. I didn't know what I could do to help. I'd brought her homeopathic medicine whenever I could find it; she'd started out calling it voodoo, but now she hungered for anything that might relieve the pain.

"Last night my leg was like a wooden board. How's a person supposed to sleep with a board attached to her body?" She looked at me as if expecting an answer.

"It's about Olivia," I began. To her, Olivia was still a girl; to the world, she was a forty-year-old lesbian raising a daughter with another woman.

"Is there any way you could get me a stronger version of those pills? Ever since I ran out, the leg gives me trouble."

She was not above shocking confessions, I knew. And I was determined. "Olivia will arrive with a woman. The woman is her lover. You'll see this when they arrive," I said.

I hadn't wanted to use the word "partners." She'd see them holding hands, kissing on the lips.

But she didn't react. Instead, she went on: "In bed at night, I lie awake for hours, thinking about surgery. I imagine the surgeon's knife severing the thing that holds my leg to my torso. All at once, I'm legless but much freer."

After her own confession, she closed her eyes as if she'd fallen asleep. I looked around her bedroom, trying to find some way to continue my disclosure. My eyes fastened on the window. It was nearly dark outside, the sky navy.

"Her lover has a grey crew-cut and piercing blue eyes. They'll walk along the beach, holding hands. Everyone will know what they are."

I'd done my best; she'd have to see for herself. Before leaving, I put my hand on her painful leg and pressed firmly. She didn't flinch.

Ovid's Songs

We'd miscalculated: Olivia's grandmother found Sappho charming, and laughed girlishly with her when they were together. In fact, she let her own blue gaze turn coquettish.

Olivia's father was the one who required comforting: he felt guilty, certain that he'd done something to make his daughter's life difficult.

Once, years ago, I tried to make a case with Olivia for my own guilt: I stole her father from her when she was only twelve. But she wouldn't hear of my absconding with her father as theft.

For the moment, the only real theft has been avoided. To this day, Olivia and I drink scotch and dance together, our own addendum to Ovid's songs.

Until We Go to Sleep

Trying to Speak

this is the letter i'd write to him:
this is the letter (i'd write)

More There Than Before

Before arriving, I expect to find him diminished. I fret and worry until I see the man I imagined halved or quartered or simply obliterated by his ill-functioning brain. But in a way, he's more present than ever, almost larger-than-life now, battling to say what he can say as he watches the words float away.

His Brain

I imagine his brain a murky river that speeds up to take away simple words or slows, allowing the sentences to be formed with graceful ease.

Key

The key went for a walk. Out behind the barn? Danced for an hour or two, drank a beer?

He found it a week later, in the tweed jacket pocket, hardly drunk, maybe hung-over, cowering, or cocky, he couldn't decide. Warm metal in his palm, liquid.

CELLS

Don't pretend you didn't know: cells can't go on living forever.

People fall apart, sometimes in front of your eyes.

COOKING

In the morning, my mother assembles ingredients, ready to bake a cake. Brown sugar coats two fingers, there's egg white in her hair. Something yellow on the floor. I watch her almost step in it, three times, before I go down on a knee at her feet, sponge in hand.

ORIGAMI

When things get bad, Hisako comes over with perfectly square sheets of colored paper and folds them before our eyes. We're thirsty for the intricate folds, the neat handling of paper. Absorbed in the motion of the hands that flick and fold, we find peace.

Soon, a line of colored boats drifts lazily across the lake of the kitchen table, floats along the river of our conversation.

After a cup of tea, Hisako gathers her things and sets off. In her wake, a gaggle of geese flies the table in a lazy V.

SLIPPERS

He came out for dinner in his slippers. She said: "I want you to promise me that you won't do that again."

He said: "No, I won't."

Very cheerfully.

THOSE THINGS

She asked: "What are those things on the table?" Thinking they were something good to eat, dessert perhaps. We saw that she was talking about his fingers. He wiggled them; we laughed.

CONSCIOUSNESS

Once, looking for a word like brain or mind, he said "what's on top." I'm still not certain he was out of words, but possibly just casting an ironic tone on the process and his situation.

WHY HIM?

My sister said: "Why did *he* have to get it? Why couldn't it be someone *else*?"

Alarmed, I asked: "Like *who*?"

JUMPING TO CONCLUSIONS

Sometimes, it's as if they're already dead.

ORPHEUS AND EURIDICE

The conversation kept getting stuck: odd silences, strange attempts to move it along.

But how *does* one say things without words when the sense of a word's departure is stronger than one's possession of it?

Like Orpheus looking back at Euridice, the word falls apart.

DOCK

Some days, one lies too much in the harbor of oneself, tied to a splintery dock, banging against the hard shallows of a life.

BAKING

Why is it that dogs always come near, sniffing *her* hands? Dogs stray from the people who fuss but warm to my mother's lack of interest.

Perhaps they smell butter on her skin. She's always baking, putting things into the oven and waiting to take them out. Cutting into cakes that have risen, letting cookies cool on racks. Carrying plates to doorsteps. Leaving them without a word, with only the lightest knock.

GLASS BEADS

Grandmother, nearly a century old, hangs on. Tack-sharp.

When she hears that you're going to Venice, she says: "Just one thing. Go through the lobby of the Gritti Palace, and find a table on the terrace along the canal. Sit there for a minute and think of me."

You return with glass beads, a raspberry and a blackberry, plop them into a thin porcelain dish.

Not missing a beat, she says: "They're yours when I'm gone."

PRE-LINGUAL

I remember the day the *word* "house" came away from the *thing* house and all it meant. I kept saying, house. House? How-s? Then word and thing sewed themselves together, the chasm temporary.

NEW YEAR'S EVE

People are out in the rain, buying next year's Christmas cards, half-priced. Where do they come by such faith?

NOT YET

The grandmother's eye that closed six months ago is open again. Fixing it on you, she says: "I'm not dead yet."

LOST STREET

They called to say: "We've lost the street where we parked the car."

The end is always just around the corner, but sometimes it seems as if the street between here and there is long and if you walk slowly enough it may go on forever.

CRACKS

Toward the end of every meal, when the rest of us are sitting with our hands in our laps, my mother says: "I'm sorry I'm taking so long."

When did she become such a slow eater?

>Step on a crack, break your mother's back.

GRAVES

Eyeing the dark soil in the yard, prepared for new plantings, she said: "I can see you've got our graves ready."

THEM

The only real *them* there is.

PREPARATION

You make them grow old, jump them across huge expanses of time, trying to prepare. Just when you've finally accepted the fact, they appear jaunty, high-spirited; you're ashamed.

KNOWLEDGE

Wanting to plumb the depths of my mind so I can know where he is when he goes there.

A COUPLE OF THINGS

She said she knows he's thinking about things he doesn't necessarily mention to her.

"How do you know?" I asked.
"He talks in his sleep," she said. "I hear him say, 'my brain'."

MIRACLES

We learn to get by, and it's always that, a denial of some greater ambition and potential. Our miracles are diminutive, but they can seem great.

"DEATH"

He said: "We'll do this until we go to sleep."

MIND READERS

When our children are small stuttering beings, trying their mouths around language, we're told not to help but to let them find the words themselves.

Should we practice the same control with our parents when, small stuttering beings once again, their tongues go around so pathetically in their mouths that we can almost picture their emptied-out minds?

We become mind-readers, supplying lost words. It's not difficult— we've lived with these people's minds in our own heads all our lives.

TURNING

It's both appalling and fascinating to watch a mind turn like this. That's the only way to think of it: a turning.

Inside

Sometimes, weird sentences run through my brain, as if he's speaking to me, from inside my head, and his logic has replaced mine.

For instance:

Because the garden was almost too wet.
His dinner the other night, and then.

Cynical

One could be utterly cynical and say: this is a fascinating inquiry into the roots of language and identity. The dissection of a real person, cell by cell.

Empty

She heard him say of an empty bag: "This bag is quiet."

She? I.

We

Fuck time to a standstill.

Quiet enough now to hear men calling, boat to boat.

Unthreading the Labyrinth

We watch their lives come undone.

Weeping

People go to church in order to weep without imposing tears on their loved ones.

FREEDOM

Is freedom simply the ability to go beyond guilt?

Or is it the knowledge that even things declared whole and done aren't finished at all?

As we finish one another's thoughts, sentences, and works of art, so we finish each others' lives.

ABSTINENCE

After a period of abstinence, I find that the swim of words and the wind of eros are located side by side.

I fall into that particular sea, the breath and buck of it. The rapid climax of wave upon wave.

MEN ON CROSSES

BREATHING

In certain weathers, Ruth knows exactly the weight of their violence: a life was taken.

But she's still in awe: the wonder of so many tiny lives saved in the destruction of that one life.

A Dr. West. Ob/Gyn. Known for his loyal service to several abortion clinics in the south.

How responsible need she hold herself for his death? A woman who pushed pamphlets into the soft hands of dazed women. Women like herself, seeking answers to insoluble problems.

Some of the women clawed at her; some cried in her arms. Others walked ahead, stony-faced. As she'd done, once.

Sometimes, at home, she can't take a deep breath and thinks of men on crosses. She knows they die of suffocation.

BLOOM

Ruth began to call the quiet bloom in her chest what others have called it for ages: God. She felt him there with her—presence, protector, companionable silence. That's when she'd first known wild-haired Samuel with his charismatic gestures. His blue eyes that held hers, and everyone's.

Like a prophet's, Samuel's beard reached halfway down his chest.
Beside him, God stayed in her view.

CHASTITY

William, she'd said, you're not to touch me for a year.

Like the good prince in a fairy tale, he arrived when she needed him
and went along with her wish. It infuriated him to see and not touch.
But she'd known something he hadn't: today, they water the daisies
in the grass, planted for the eventuality of a child.

SELF-ABUSE

William's been trying to piece it together.

"Was it a question of abuse?"

No, she wasn't abused, at least not that she can remember.

"But," she says, "as you know, I'm good at slitting my consciousness
into so many layers and tributaries that I'm no longer quite of this
world. That's self-abuse, wouldn't you say?"

He can't disagree.

"The things that save me? A pebble on the road, the density of the
sky, hunger pangs. The thought of children's bodies, curved into
sleep. Their quiet, even breath."

She'd once said: "Words can't help. They become wind or competing
voices that bind me in a conundrum."

William is still not sure how to take any of this, sometimes pictures himself running into the desert until the small blot of him
disappears.

GHOST

She'd aborted a baby, once. Though no one in the clinic had told her the sex of the embryo, she'd *felt* it was a boy. Then, when she'd first seen the child, it *was* a boy.

A boy walking along the pavement, he looked at her until she looked back, then skipped over and took her hand. Counting back, she'd figured that he was five.

After that, she'd seen him riding a bicycle and swimming in a lake. It always took a second for her to recognize him—he grew between visits.

When Ruth described her moments with the boy, William couldn't help but imagine it. Once he'd seen the boy in his own imagination, he couldn't undo what he'd seen.

HER GOAT

William asks: "Did it really begin with the goat?"

As a child, her chore had been to milk it. The morning she forgot to, her father left the skinned carcass hanging from the rafters. He'd aimed to teach perfection.

"It began with my father. The goat was only a step along the way."

RESPONSIBILITY

A Dr. West? *A*? One of how many? There must have been tens of thousands of Doctors West in the United States of America. She knows he had a wife and children (three boys).

She knew then, too.

Samuel had led them forth.

HER

She loved him but there were days, even now, when she wanted a guarantee that she could keep the color from bleeding outside the lines.

This child: the start of something new? Or the greatest disaster of her life?

THAT JESUS

What was that Jesus about? How did it suckle her?

William put up with the Jesus thing because he was afraid she couldn't be without it.

His constant thought: With the birth of their child, maybe she'll throw Jesus over her shoulder, walk on without him.

He never said Jesus was bad. But one day he told her that it made her look *away from* when she could have been looking *at*.

FACE PAINTED ON WOOD

It's not just that you recognize him but, more important, he *knows* you. What's the tenor of this recognition? (How can she avoid such sightings?)

For a beat, she lets herself be bathed in the gaze of a Jesus painted on old wood.

Then, her husband—warm, quick—merges with the painted man. The two blend into one: alive.

BLUE SCARF

He watched her knit a stream of blue scarf.

SHARDS

He holds onto shards, trying to learn. She's vitally lose-able.

He looks out at the desert through the window, holds the constellation of saguarro, sand, and sky as if in his hands, not as souvenir but as talisman. He doesn't understand what it is to lean on Jesus but he wants her to be strong.

He tells her: "Remember what you have. Good soil, enough water, pancakes, ceiling-high bookshelves, a comfortable chair. Me," careful to focus his gaze on a distant point.

TELLING HIM

She refused to name the cult. He tried to guess until she told him not to.

Naked together one afternoon, she held his hand, forcing him to jump into the river with her. Unprepared, his jump was clumsy. Submerged, grace was restored. They swam long strokes, passing tall trees that seemed to be moving in the opposite direction but were, they both knew, absolutely still.

Then she told him.

DEFINED

William reads aloud: "Joseph Conrad described terrorists as 'fools victimized by ideas they cannot possibly believe...while they mouth slogans or even practice anarchist beliefs, their motives are the result of self-display, power plays, class confusion, acting out roles.'"

"Jesus Christ was a terrorist?"
"No, *Samuel* was. Is."

He's due to leave prison the month their baby's supposed to come.

POSSESSIONS

Ruth told him there was a period of intense worship and prayer when she gave up all her possessions, handed over birthday checks from her grandmother as well as hair clips, photographs of her sister, and even a half-eaten bag of Gummy Bears. Nothing was her own. In exchange, she was *theirs*, a possession of the diamond-hard jewel "*us*."

Once Samuel was behind bars, she pickled olives and sold them by the side of the road. Weather-worn, lost.

William appeared, selling tomatoes across the way.

MAN ON A CROSS

Here in the desert, she picks up things that remind her of parts of herself. Bone. Sand. Nothing liquid unless she's out before sunrise.

The desert saves her marriage once, twice, and then she wants to think it may be Jesus. It's the sixth month and she's desperate to tell William. She circles around him with the need to say it.

William thinks: a man on a cross, nails through his ankles and wrists. How difficult are carpenter skills? He hopes he's given her a boy to even out some wrongness in her. Fears it'll come out a girl, complicated.

DOLLS

For a year or more, when the olives were gone, she made soft dolls with pinpoint eyes and yarn hair, their mouths permanently shut.

SEEDLINGS

Her husband comes in with dirt on his hands, in his hair and eyelashes. After they've eaten together in silence, she dares to look again at the face painted on wood. The eyes look toward a distance she can only begin to fathom.

The next morning, she plants olive seedlings, though people tell her they're illegal.

How can a tree be illegal, she wonders. Who decides?

Seven months. Her belly is high, round, and hard.

"Dad?"

"Dad, are you there?"

In the expanse beyond their house, farther than she will ever allow her unborn child to venture. An inexhaustible place. Rocky, bright with shadow on this Tuesday morning. She's left him at home, sleeping.

Desperate not to lose it, she offers it to God. "Take it, please." "Please," she says, loudly, knowing her voice is tiny, inaudible. A syllable hovering above the dryness of bones.

"Dad?"

She Thinks

An unborn person is no less than me. And: How could I have done that?

Praying

Jesus comes back to her in the eighth month. She wakes up with the taste of him in her mouth.

That freezing morning, she picks up stones in the desert. A stone for each prayer, then one for each word. Jesus speaks to her in whispers.

Walking out to find her, William seems to caress the air between them. For a split second, he's Samuel.

The Desert

So much of what one sees in the desert *looks dead* but isn't.

THE BRIGHTEST PART OF HERSELF

Her fear that she could ditch it all, chuck everything, offer her life in exchange for something certain. Those people who wore cheap tennis shoes when they committed communal suicide. Thought they were on their way to heaven. As if tennis or any kind of shoes were necessary.

When she thinks in the brightest part of herself, she knows there's nothing but this, right here. Sometimes, she can't take the fact of finality. Tries to find ways around it. Philosophical trinkets, religious knick-knacks.

Her body tells the real story: nine months.

THE REAL STORY

She was once in love with an abortion terrorist. Eventually she realized that what he did had very little to do with saving unborn babies and almost everything to do with his stockpiles of violence.

Someone once said that the moral content of a violent act was determined by the purpose of the act.

In the desert behind their house, she looks into a deep pink sky, sees the clear shape of the mountains going on forever and realizes that she no longer believes in the morality of violence.

She knows from warring with herself that violence only begets more violence.

The sky becomes so dark that if she hadn't been standing in her own backyard, she'd never have made it back inside the house.

CHILDBIRTH

William looks into her eyes when the pain threatens to take her away. He waits to see the moment when life becomes itself, the first breath.

Together, the three of them breathe against the terror of suffocation. She's given birth to something bigger than them both, immense: a tiny wriggling child. Their son's face is a rose, opening and closing with the declaration of his wants. He makes it seem easy.

SAMUEL

He's out of prison and walking the same streets. Some days, child burrowing into her, she trembles with the thought that he could already be on his way. It's not the violence she fears but the charisma of his certainty.

There are days when she knows she'd walk away from her life, her husband, her child without going back inside for a jacket or her wallet.

DESERT

A mound of desert in each palm, she watches the light abandon the land. Color leaves in increments too small to measure, but today she's been given special sight.

In the moment before stars pierce the dark, she lets sand drain from her fingers, listens as snakes slither, lizards dash. She hears the rocks groan like old men settling, the shifting of sand, she hears the sigh of the desert creatures wakening to the night.

Then it's time to go back inside, watch the small face nuzzle toward the self it's becoming. She waits for her husband's arrival, trembling.

He inhales deeply, holds it. Poised, unbreathing, he leaves as much of the world to her as he can. Some days, he goes outside to exhale to save her from breathing in what he's already used.

INFINITY

But—was it a doll or a person, or both? And, who could say? The girls, I guess, who read the stories, or the mothers who read them to the little girls who couldn't.

DOLL TO GIRL

Pauline once told me that writing the Robin Stories was so easy, it was as if they wrote themselves.

Robin was sometimes a doll, sometimes a girl. Girl to doll, the hair stiffened and turned slightly darker. Doll to girl, her lips tingled, her heart beat fiercely against her chest.

The adults required her to be both and while she didn't mind being either, she wanted to be a girl when *she* wanted to be, and a doll as well on her own terms, not theirs.

GIRL TO DOLL

Robin, the girl, cut the doll's hair first, and then her own long, never-sheared curls. The girl was beaten silly; the doll lay in her cradle, pretending inertia but actually planning the next caper.

POROUS

The wall between them was membrane-thin and porous. As a girl, she could be shut out of the doll's life from one minute to the next. When a doll, the girl often turned and walked off without a glance.

Sunbathing Lions

This is what I understood: the girl's world—the large apartment furnished with upright, always-judging chairs, cabinets, tables, the city's yellowed light—penetrated the doll's world with its dangerous rivers and plateaus where lions sunbathed, and the sky was red, even at noon.

The Danger in Dolls

For thirty years now, the doctors have assured Pauline that she's not to blame, but there are times when she's certain that such frequent crossing of lines has left her this way, split.

I don't know; I never played with dolls.

Death

Now my husband says Pauline is dying, but he can't seem to tell me of what. Can one die of madness?

Are the girl and the doll dying, too?

Madhouse

There were empty years when the doll and the girl changed places without rhythm or logic, increasing speed until Pauline couldn't locate or know herself, and the doll, usually happy if a little dazed, had the upper hand.

I'd imagine that Pauline, the woman, in and out of madhouses her whole life, despised the doll, or perhaps merely coveted her place in the world. Being real and feeling unreal must be worse than being unreal and feeling real. Or are they equally untenable, if in different ways? Poor Robin. Poor Pauline.

ENVY

For years, I envied Pauline her Robin, that pink-red bloom of madness.

TODAY

Pauline lies as if comatose for hours, hardly able to rouse herself to smoke, then does, sitting up, and exhaling in Robin's direction. Robin gets up, of course, to open a window. But has to stand there guarding it in case Pauline is suddenly overcome by the desire to jump.

SHARING

In their younger days, very little marked the girl from the doll. They shared ice cream cones, built castles at the beach, and examined baby boys beneath their diapers. Their clothes, of different sizes, were almost the same.

In cogent moments, Pauline wonders if this burdensome love for something invented is what unbalanced her mind. Her desire was always to be *more*, but a shared more—didn't Robin gain, too, from being imagined by the woman, Pauline?

Here, lucidity stops. Robin enters her mind, inhabits her.

Termites, glass, knives, fire—these are some of the words Pauline used to describe how it felt when Robin broke loose, spilling the contents of her mind.

The Robin Stories, a task she wished she'd left un-started. By then, wishing was so mixed in with the fundamentals of eating that she confused food and thought, pizza and Niagara Falls (a place she'd never been), milk and everything else she'd ever known.

DOUBT

Sometimes I doubt the book, the doll, the way Pauline said the doll's rubberized body came to life, filling her hands with sparks of numbness. That quickening, the only child Pauline would ever have.

I

By the time I met her, the book was out of print. But as I wanted the man I'd seen kissing her, so I wanted a copy for myself.

I wanted to hold the book in my hand: a done deal. Instead I was offered a story that felt too close to home.

KISSING

Before I ever kissed him, I watched the two of them kiss just beyond a doorway. I'd recently arrived in a country foreign to me, native to them, looking to begin the rest of my life.

I can't say what I was looking for, only that I wanted what was there, beyond the doorframe, exposed.

I wanted to be *her* in that scene, the way she'd once wanted to be a girl in a book.

In the end, she lost track of the book that held her image. I walked into that scene and remade it entirely.

SHADOWS

When they kissed, in a brightly lit apartment, their bodies threw shadows. I've always thought it was their feelings I saw, as if their history were visible.

Perhaps that vision was the entrance fee. Two weeks hadn't passed before I was kissing the man. But our kissing was shadow-less. The heat that emanated from us went between us, and around us, entering places I hadn't known existed. If there was any shadow, it went out into the future, perhaps toward this moment now.

The Now of Kissing

We still kiss, in a place without shadows. The now of kissing, tongues fencing, dispels them.

Sometimes it's almost as if we're in a book. But not hers, *never* hers. The book she wrote was for children. Still it was, for her, a book that took courage to write.

His book and mine are written in time, in gestures and children, acts and trees.

But her book can't be dismissed. Even if it's out of print, I dream it into existence, awakening sometimes with the feeling that I'm holding it.

Out of Print

Visiting her empty house last summer, I wanted simply to put the book back on the shelf. But as I've said, the book is out of print.

There was no simple way to get rid of her: the agonizing madness of her existence, her desire to jump from high places, the need to pay burly men to stand guard, just in case. The almost empty cutlery drawer (tens of tiny spoons, her only friends). Chipped paint, cracked walls, a buckling ceiling. Notes written in almost-illegible handwriting, glued or taped to the wall above where she slept. Notes I didn't want to read, but read anyway.

I found no answers. Nothing titillating or even precise. Just a litany of dates, numbers, names. Grocer, psychiatrist, hospital, pharmacist. The ones who keep her tied, nominally, to the earth.

I expected to but didn't find his name there.

DEPARTURE

I never played with dolls as a child, couldn't believe they were anything but rubber and glass. Pauline infiltrated the membrane between our world and that of the dolls but once there, she never really came back.

INFINITY

She lived as a small boat on an immense body of water, battered by weather, too far from shore. Shivering with sunstroke and dehydration, she was a body alone, a mind spinning in isolation.

Pauline's life is a case of infinity. I have no other understanding of the term.

Here, I leave thoughts of her unfinished and lay her to rest, like a book put down in the middle because after all, it isn't the book you were once so eager to read.

EROS

This genius sees what's small in the galaxy beyond our atmosphere, sees from here to there and back again and taking his vision onto the nerves of his body, lets others see what he sees.

This is genius, ever a version of eros.

SHARING A TELESCOPE

Someone else: a minor for another two months and six days. A someone else eager to see what *he* could see, a minor who put his eye against the telescope when it was still warm from his own. That was the first heat they shared.

CAKE

His parents note that prison is reconstructing him: once stocky and short, he's now wiry. Near the others, he's merely small, not a good choice here where the men are tougher than any he'd ever imagined.

Boys were his delectation; girls, always an option.

His sex life, a smorgasbord of the cake and the eating of it.
Until now.

ROBBERY

He thinks the genesis of his crime is greed. Are some people more omnivorous than others?

For years, he was taken too seriously; now, he's a number and an asshole. Even though he knew enough to tell them he was in for robbery.

The Perfect Crime

He thinks about the perfect crime and knows he's reached a limit when he sees himself killing his parents in order to stop them from making him.

X-ray Vision

After a few weeks, he's become so sensitive to everything unspoken that he knows which men have killed. As if he's observing through a microscope, he knows what's happening inside each one of these men, and never lets down his guard.

Options

The free circulation of air at his back is not an option.

Plagiarism

The only other time he messed up was for plagiarizing a friend's homework. Not an exam, test, or even a quiz. Just the homework.

The first step on the slippery road?

#

Here he is, in prison, #_____, less man than number, except when they're together, eating or walking in the yard. Then, he stands alone. Fear springs him a life.

SHANK

He knows what a shank is, that they're made using various ingredients in the basement shop. He's heard that one made of paper went straight through the skin of a little guy in for armed robbery and rape. It seems an odd mixture but he's learning the mixtures are practically infinite.

Is this really his country? Is he really here?

CONSTELLATIONS

He's always been propelled toward the stars.

Now, he makes his own constellations, each beam of light a man. He memorizes the constellations, and knows when a star is out of place.

ALL MAPS ARE INTERNAL

All maps, he discerns, are internal.

If he'd walked a different path, clung to the cliff.
But the nerves on his skin sang a frenetic tune; he couldn't resist the call of gravity.
He jumped.
And was apprehended at the bottom, a swift sigh.

HE, A BALL

Once a star in a constellation, now he's a ball in a pinball machine with nothing but a loony gravity to carry him.

He wills himself a particular essence of gravity, waiting out the days, the court proceedings; he tries to pray.

If it had been a girl, none of this would've happened.

He Pictures Himself Centaur

Monsters, like maps, are internal, but his country's forgotten, or still hasn't learned what's private. He pictures himself centaur, looks down at his hooves.

Just Noise

Cell doors bang, keys clang, hoarse voices shout. No songs here, just noise.

He resists the temptation to make a song of this cacophony. Doing so could keep him here forever.

His Mother

His mother brings her lovely aging face that he must prepare himself to see. The familiarity of it tears him down to boy, something he mustn't be here where anything boy is hurt.

Flag

It happened in a stall, his head held so tightly against their biceps that afterwards, his neck hurt more than his asshole which was not exactly virginal.

He hid the bleeding with torn paper, knew the red of it was a bright flag.

Sleep

Coming out of something he called sleep, his hands were fisted, his feet hurt as if he'd walked miles in the wrong shoes.

RAPE

It was doubly shameful, an insult to anything he might have thought of as integrity—that place had once given him pleasure. So this is rape, he thinks, and knows a different version of women.

RUST

Everything here is rusty; water or some other liquid eats away at things. Nothing shines or sparkles. Knowing that this ugliness is a mirror of himself, he takes another bite of something white and bland.

PANIC

On the other side, this would be called a panic attack.

He lets his heart beat as if it would remove itself from his body.

MUSIC

In a pocket of the long, never-dark, never-silent night, there's a tune he knows but can't bring forth. Its beauty sickens him, epitomizes everything he must resist.

At the same time, this unsung tune holds him together in a way more visceral than bones and muscle.

How many more days? Nights? Noons? Shadows?

PINPOINT

If he's a genius, it's because he's learned to pull inside himself everything that could've been showing. This is being vacuum-packed, a pinpoint in the universe. (No longer a star.)

BEING BLACK

Within minutes of meeting M., I knew that I needed him as a friend. He was gay, out, and in his thirties. Over the next few months, in an indirect way, I helped him find a release from his agoraphobia. I figured he owed me one.

Once he'd flown across the Atlantic, twice, and knew he was capable of going anywhere in the world, I opened the conversation with a line I'd been thinking about for a while. I said: "The closest I'll ever come to being black is having a gay son."

M.

He's fine-boned, dark-skinned, eager. His mind has wings. His heart sits high in the region of his throat. Heart and mind jam and bounce, race.

I've never seen him calm. His body doesn't tremble but vibrates to keep pace with his brain. It's impossible to be bored in his company.

NEUTER

M. said that the altar of his father's church was neutered but I wonder if he meant neutral, and is there a difference, anyway?

The altar of a church should be neutral and if it's not, perhaps it should be neutered.

But is that what he meant?

JESUS MAKES HIM LAUGH

He's drawn to the church, though of course it's not just any church but his father's church, or the Church of his father.

Jesus provides something, a long-haired dead man, supposedly alive, to think about when nothing else is funny; Jesus makes him laugh. But, too, he takes Jesus seriously, in his own pagan way.

After so many hours of Sunday Mass with his father the priest intoning the words, he can't help but know it by heart. Ancient-ish words that have always been in his nighttime dreams and his erotic bubbles.

The appurtenances of religion are his; feeling has leaked away. He likes nothing more than listening to one of the great divas sing Verdi or Wagner, dressed in satin and feathers, and always alone.

A HIT SONG

No one would call him a rarified, cut-off man. There are few on the street more engaging. Children love him, even if he's slightly terrified of them. Cats brush against him, dogs jump up to lick his face.

He's a friend to women.

A star. A hit song. An immaculate influence. He's never held a gun or a horse's reins.

His purity isn't innocent but kind. He loves the earth, the sky, his father's religious robes.

The things he's shunned (because he saw that they shunned him): his mother's many silver tubes of lipstick, her glass bottles of perfume, her dresses and high-heeled shoes. The curl of her pageboy.

He collects old 78s, religious paraphernalia, autographed pictures of pre-60s stars. The collections take up so much room in his apartment that he's not quite sure what to do.

On the Warpath

He keeps his hair long on the sides, short enough on top to make himself laugh when he looks: it could be the start of a mohawk. He's on the warpath, but one of his own choosing. How to get from here to there? Or, more likely in his case, from there to here? He wants respect. Refuses to understand sneers. No curled lips or rolled eyes. He'll keep his hands in gloves with pearl clasps, pull no punches, as long as you look him in the eye when you tell him you hate faggots.

Because he knows you can't do it, not if you're really looking at him, lips naturally cherry, green eyes beneath lashes in no need of thickener urging you to see clearly, perhaps for the very first time.

A Tortured Life

He tells me that shame has lodged itself in his mother. Because she was raised not to have or want a self, her desires are those of a now-imagined community. She left the old country behind but it won't leave her. This is all she knows; a tortured life.

Discussing her, M. and I imagine her taking some small solace from another woman, perhaps even a cousin. A hand on her hand. A finger to her cheek.

He's the storm that came of their coupling. A thing he prefers not to think about. A distasteful thing. "Gross," he says, as if he's still fifteen.

His Mother

She sewed their clothes. A display of thrift, skill, and honor. Imperiousness.

Homespun, her sword?

THREADBARE

His father sits alone, a rock, but a glorious rock. Always himself. This is how men are.

Some of the sons come loose like torn fabric, threads unravel. They stitch themselves up as they may, with skills learnt of watching their mothers. The fathers may be threadbare but their stitches are always knotted.

It's the mothers who are constantly sewing themselves up and tearing themselves apart.

THE FATHER,

a Father. With a bright-toned singing voice, a voice everyone coveted and hired to accompany their children's baptisms, marriages, the congregants' funerals.

I've never heard this particular voice, though I've heard others intone notes on the same scale.

(—EVER?)

She is a woman I'm relieved to be able to distance myself from, to say: she is there and I am here. Nothing overlaps.

But then again, even if I never sewed my children's clothes, even if I still sleep with my husband and am affectionate with him in public, there are parts in any two mothers, any two women, that overlap.

(He doesn't remember his parents touching—*ever?*)

BELOVED

He covets photographs of his mother from when she was young and lovely, and can't abide the disjunction between this loveliness and her subsequent hard-bitten angularity. To abide it would be to accept his loss, not just of his mother but of the young boy he once was, beloved.

Religion's Her soup,

her family, her tide. She washes in it and sleeps there, but never anymore beside her husband, the priest.

But what are her *wishes*? Is there any kind of prayer left in her? (Was there ever?)

Into the Night

His ties to his siblings are loose, at best. Stabilized by anger.

This is the last thing he says before he asks for one more glass of water, and we hug quickly, and he runs down the stairs, unlocks his bike, then takes off into the night.

Sushi

The next time we meet, this time at the sushi restaurant down the street, he begins by telling me that we're all always waiting to become what we aren't, what we hardly dare imagine: the life that comes at us in flickers, the underside of God's robe, the worn part that usually goes unseen.

I don't disagree.

Passed Photographs

M. is neither an artist nor a maker of children. He's brimming with energy and intelligence, and yet there's no objectified form his gift can take.

He is a lover of men.

He would possibly tell you that his mother messed him up for life. More likely, though, he'd tell you of the exquisite, if entirely too feminine clothes she sewed for him—some by hand, others on the old Singer. Clothes most boys would've refused to wear; clothes he's wearing in photographs he still passes around.

(But clandestinely. And only to close friends.)

RECYCLING NOSTALGIA

He wants to go back to the years before he turned fifteen, when he wasn't bothered by the growing awareness of certain verities. "Before that," he says, "the family was perfect, harmonious." At least, that's how it looks to him now.

So he asks: "How do I get rid of my nostalgia?" And: "What am I supposed to do with it?"

He looks at me, across the table.

How am I supposed to say that, like a sturdy child, it's something he'll never give away or leave alone?

ELEPHANTS

It's a few months later that we finally have the conversation I've been waiting for.

We talk about the elephant in the room that no one will acknowledge. He finds it outrageous, or at least incomprehensible, that my son won't say the word.

I tell him that sometimes the elephant in a room is so obvious and accepted—commenting would be ridiculous.

But I understand his point. Things do need to be *said*. In the meantime, my son and I will enjoy our energetic ramble through the mirror that says: I know that you know that I know. On and on.

Perhaps it's this bit of infinity, an awful lot like nostalgia, that neither of us wants to desecrate. M. probably wouldn't disagree.

Anthropology

Participant Observer:

My first two days here on the island, no one recognizes me. I've achieved invisibility, ordinarily no mean feat. In this place where I lived and loved thirty years ago, I expect to be seen. Instead, I watch and see.

There's the same wide bay, the boats rocked by steady water, but almost everything else has changed. The buildings along the harbor are higher and the people, too, much taller.

Have I shrunk? Have my peers given birth to a generation of fortified giants? If Vasilis and I had had children, would they too have been taller than both their parents?

Critical Eye:

I, the anthropologist, follow the flight of a rumor, watch it become gossip, finally lodging in a fold of the Panayia's blue-painted garment in the icon hanging beside Jesus in the church on the hill. Thirty years earlier, I wouldn't have believed it possible: an answer found in an icon? What could the Virgin Mary possibly have to say to me?

Field Notes:

The residents see that I have the same kind of notebook I used to carry: black cardboard covers, a rubber band closing it.

The pleasure of these pages, I think. The fact of their existence.

But when the life is gone, what value the pages?

BEHAVIORS:

In the old days, they'd ask for my Bic just when I wanted to use it. I'd let go of the pen, and the thought. Eventually I developed a shorthand, using images in alphabetical order. *Apple, balloon, cup*: An apple sat in Stavroula's hand, reminding me to note that she was fourteen when her father married her off to her second cousin, Manolis.

Now at the end of each day, I send everything I've recorded to a rented niche in cyberspace. I imagine a clean, dark place, somewhere I'd like to sit on hot days.

OBJECTIVITY:

As a young woman, I strived for objectivity. My notes coalesced into a thesis that later became a book and was published. I wrote about the dowry system as it was experienced by the people living on the island.

Today, objectivity seems beside the point. My notes, helter-skelter, combine chaff and wheat. One can't know what's important until the end—of the field work, the affair, the book, the life.

META-NARRATIVE:

On a feast day, the Dormition, I dressed in a skirt and sandals, pulled my hair back, slipped pen and paper into a small purse. I followed the townspeople along the dusty, hot road to a chapel on the other side of the island. We were a long line of pilgrims, in August.

I wasn't interested in their forms of worship; to me, every icon looked the same. I wanted to understand the island's dowry system, and my goal (I see now) was neither scientific nor objective. How, I remember thinking, can a woman be equated with goods? How considered a possession?

Then one day I let myself be possessed by a man. This had very little to do with his desire to possess, and much to do with me. When I found myself in Vasilis' arms, I knew I'd crossed a boundary. Actually, I thought I'd penetrated the culture. A short-lived euphoria: within hours, everyone knew, and no eyes would look into mine. The oldest women spat on the road. Overnight I was alone, accompanied only by a nerve-wracking sexual hum.

Deep Structures of Society:

After giving myself to him like that, the only way I could hold my life together, I thought, was by accepting his offer of marriage. Once we'd married, I was accepted. I wore his great-grandmother's *vera*, her gold band, on the ring finger of my right hand. From where we stood, high above the harbor, we saw fourteen gold domes and blue water all the way to the next island. I knew I loved him; I knew it wouldn't last.

Female:

There are mistakes so ill-timed they can ruin a life. Still, bodies will have their say.

Metaphor:

Married, I sat with the women in damp, cold rooms, pushing embroidery needles through muslin. The women accumulated cupboards full of linens; I couldn't imagine what they'd do with so much. In their company, I never stopped feeling like an imposter. But those afternoons turned out to be like a dowry: the wealth of our conversations remains.

I came to the marriage empty-handed; when I left, I'd amassed notes toward a book, a kind of dowry.

ISSUES OF WRITING:

If I acted as a spy, it was because I wanted to help the women improve their lives. "Improve": a word I may have used in the past.

Whose life improved? Whose impoverished?

There's no spying on anyone's life but your own.

COHERENT, STABLE SELF:

One afternoon I went to the *tama* seller and bought a large, flattened tin image of a baby. I was purposely ostentatious with my purchase, pretending to be someone I wasn't: a married woman determined to bring a child into the world.

Then I went to the Virgin Mary's church and crossed myself three times before her icon. The glass enclosing her blue robe was smeared with the lipstick of worshippers. I hung the *tama* beside the others— tin outlines of hands, feet, hearts.

Everyone was convinced I was trying to become pregnant. There were plenty of days when I fooled myself.

I left at four, one hot summer morning, my notes stuffed haphazardly into my knapsack. I left my clothes, the bedding I'd purchased, a good pair of sandals. All my jewelry but the ring, the *vera*.

Over the years, I've become expert in recognizing the many forms barrenness can take: days spent in tedious conversation with oneself. The habit of resisting all paths but the one leading to cool, dark rooms.

FACTS:

I gave up my children in order to pursue my career. It's not that I gave them away: I never had any.

Theoretical Insights:

What, in fact, did I do? Enact my notions about womanhood with an innocent villager? Fall in love? After I left him, Vasilis went to another island, quickly found another woman, and married her. Now he has four grown daughters with daughters of their own.

Where is that man whose body told mine things I'd never heard before, nor (regrettably) since?

I keep reminding myself that I'm sixty—not an age for desire.

It's only these written words that steady me, calm my frantic heart.

Breaking Down Boundaries:

I thought of buying a paper icon from the armless woman who keeps vigil beside the fish market, then this Virgin blew over and landed at my feet. These small miracles.

Diachronic:

Cell phones are part of the national uniform. And women smoke now, in public. Everyone orders cappucino, cold or hot.

Phone to phone, they reach across the water and gather Vasilis home.

I don't recognize him. He's older than he was, younger than I'd imagined him. I offer him the book I've written, with a dedication I'd already penned in my office at the university.

Do any of his daughters know English? (I always knew I was writing for somebody's daughters, but I didn't realize it was for his.) On the title page, below my name, I add "How is a book like a baby?" in both languages.

After some chitchat and a coffee, we kiss on both cheeks, like friends, and go our separate ways. The rest of the day, I'm beside myself with grief.

My emotion for him has been dead for decades; it's my life I mourn.

Vow:

The taxi driver crosses himself as he maneuvers the old car on the twisting road to the church. We come perilously close to the edge several times. I don't cross myself but promise to light a candle to the Virgin.

The *vera* is as gold as it was when his great-grandmother wore it. It's in a tiny wrapped parcel, somewhere in storage in New Jersey. Or: It's been planted in the earth.

How is a book like a ring? A ring like a heart? A heart like a dowry chest full of blankets? How is a lace-edged embroidered sheet like a marriage?

Miracle:

Is it the fact of making a vow? Or the way the mind empties out during that second when the flame flares?

Superior Claims to Truth:

With words as my dowry, I stand before you.

Panagia, I am here. Take me.

Her Dowry

Daughter

Did he insist on building a church above our house because I'd failed to bear him a daughter?

Once the mold for the foundation was built, the cement poured, he turned to the details of decoration. To my mind, they were excruciatingly complicated: an icon of *this* saint, not that one, the gold leaf covering so much of each plaque of wood, the right incense-burner, the stand for the prayer books. If it were a live girl, his church, she wouldn't be able to breathe under so much decoration, so many gold baubles, not to mention the incessantly burning candles, the clouds of incense.

Where is she, this daughter, amidst so much? Of course real girls, women of all ages, are banned from going behind the *tabla*. There, the bones of a saint are sealed into the Holy Table with myrrh and frankincense, beeswax. Symbolic of Jesus' tomb, covered in a linen shroud, no one but a bishop is allowed to remove it.

In view of this new religiosity, perhaps it's better that I never bore him a girl.

Beets

The space between the priest's long front teeth had grown in the year since we'd last seen him. Together with the trusting and mysterious blue of his eyes, it gave him a saintly look. That day we served beetroot along with goat because, every other time, he'd very gently refused the meat. In the Orthodox calendar, there's always a reason to refuse animal flesh.

As he ate, the white of those two prong-like tusks was dyed by the beets. He spoke of the saints, the necessity of procuring a bone to inaugurate the little church on the hill behind the house. We kept our heads down. Finally he wiped his mouth and, noticing the magenta stain on the white napkin, drank a big gulp of wine. The magenta of the priest's teeth made me suddenly interested in Jesus, though only superficially: I wouldn't have given up the slow-roasted kid for any saint but I ate delicately, trying to show him that not all foreigners and Jews were evil. My husband, always sure of himself, tore the meat away from the bones with vigor and some violence.

MEN IN BLACK

A long line of men dressed in gowns, or *rasa* as those long black garments are called, trailed up the steep stone path strewn right and left with dwarf chrysanthemum plants. Between the long-garmented men was my husband—I couldn't help wondering how he'd gotten there. Rather than turn away, I watched the men climb until they rounded the bend and were out of sight. Even without seeing them, I knew they'd arrived at the church.

I reminded myself that there were higher points on the land, and many higher points in the world—a church would not be the apex of my life, or of our life together. This day of consecration was just one more day, a particularly tedious one with its heat and the many murmuring voices asking for water and coffee and tea and another pair of scissors and a list with names of the dead and a pot with pungent beeswax and the ever-present long garments of long-haired men, their hair greasy and bundled into knots beneath tall black hats.

Sunglasses

His cousin Irene would tell you herself: it was stupid to have taken off her sunglasses. She'd removed them because it seemed ridiculous to be wearing dark glasses in the candlelit *naos*.

The Bishop's sloppy myrrh-shaking hit her directly in the eyes, burning them. One of the villagers murmured, "You're blessed!" There was awe and some envy in the voice.

Someone handed her a tissue and she held it against shut eyes. "It was much worse than a mere sting," she said.

The villagers advised her to wear dark glasses, assuring her that the pain would soon disappear. Then, they said, having passed through a dark time, her sight would be more clear than ever, truly radiant.

Icons

Inside the church, priests chanted, incense wafted.

The carefully painted icons were all made to pattern, nothing unique but the possible addition of a little blue here in the folds of the Virgin's drapery—and nothing deviating even slightly in the way a face took form.

I saw myself smashing them one by one, ruining the pretty sheer surfaces, the prescribed colors.

My husband would be the first to declare there was an iconoclast in me, going back, he'd say, to Abraham.

Holy Room of the Lost Jews

The only other Jew on the island, our friend Mr. Jacob collected funds to renovate the dilapidated synagogue. For more than fifty years, it had been in a ramshackle state. He wanted to make it sacred again.

Three years later, he invited everyone to see the product of his effort. The building was truly magnificent, the stone smooth and clean, the dome a personal invitation from God.

Inside, they all looked up, expecting to see the usual Jesus. But the dome was empty—just an inverted cup. They crossed themselves in shock and fear. Later, Mr. Jacob himself sang, in a nasal voice, a wretched version of Byzantine chant. The Orthodox kept their fingers in a perpetual cross beneath their coats, but all the men, having succumbed, wore black-stitched beanies. Mr. Jacob explained that it was a signal to his God, notifying Him to look down. Mr. Dimitris warmed to the idea but his old lady frowned.

"We're doing this," he whispered, "for the dead. Remember old Benyahu? Here one day, selling shoes at the port, and gone the next. And his five children, their spouses and all sixteen grandchildren? Off in the *Elli* that summer, torpedoed accidentally by the Brits."

Mr. Dimitris adjusted the beanie on his bald head and continued whispering. "Think of the *Elli* going down that hot calm June day. Think of the chickens pecking among the stones all those years. And stop making that absurd little cross into your pocket, woman!"

He wasn't the only one whose half-blind eyes leaked tears in the holy room of the lost Jews.

THEOLOGIA

Theologia's nunly joy was tangible. As if reciting, she said:

"After awakening in the dark at three-thirty, the nuns pray until eight, then break for a meal. We eat for ten minutes; when a bell is rung, we may drink water.

"While we eat, one of the sisters reads from the *Lives of the Saints* so the pleasure of eating is minimized and doesn't keep us from our aim, which is to become saintly, to let our spirits go out toward God."

She smiled as she explained, as if she understood how unbelievable it would sound to us. Her eyes behind their black frames were both patient and exhilarated.

We were eager to understand the parts of a life that couldn't be put into words; it was both a relief and a small disappointment to hear someone say these things.

Before handing us bags of homegrown tangerines and sending us on our way, the nun left us with an intriguing statement: "Simple beauty," the nun said, "shortens the distance between eye and soul."

CONVERSATION WITH AN ICONOGRAPHER

The iconographer's face was covered with dark moles. She was at least a hundred pounds overweight.

The icons she painted, she said, were hardly her own, but something that came from God: it came through her and out onto the piece of wood. It's not that she disappeared, exactly, while painting. She was aware of herself, but faintly. Occasionally, someone stood nearby, watching her. That presence was her self.

Icon painters follow a formula, adding their own touches in only the subtlest ways. She was free to change the color of the Virgin's robe, but could never deviate from red or blue. "It's a small choice," she said, "but sufficient."

CONVERSION

One doesn't think very often or pointedly about a priest's body, particularly if he's an old priest. When I saw the abbot that morning, crossing the narrow road between the monastery and the chicken coop, I thought he saw my car. But perhaps he was thinking of God or one of Jesus' miracles. The car just tapped him, but he went over at once in a kind of tumble. When I stopped the car and got out, he was on the ground, face down.

He looked like a blackened marshmallow with just a little white knot of hair. The wall-eyed monk, Isidoros, waddled over from where he was feeding the monastic fowl: geese, ducks, chickens, peacocks. Bending down so his *rasa* hiked up and the soles of his black shoes were visible, he spoke to the abbot, Pater Chrysanthos, while I waited, standing nearby but not too close.

Isidoros' lame eyes were purple. Almost a pet himself, he was the keeper of the animals in the small world of the monastery. He recited the Lord's Prayer with a stutter. Listening, I felt as if birds had gotten inside my ears, their wings flapping. All three peacocks strutted, colors fanned, toward the traffic jam.

I didn't know what to say. *Pater, are you all right?*

His black skullcap had been knocked off his head; limp white hair was held back by a piece of string. Isidoros looked like a gigantic crow helping the abbot to his feet. I took a few steps forward and facing him, reached out—not for his hand, he'd think I wanted to kiss it— but for his arm, clad in worn black material. From close up, I saw the fabric had been mended many times, with tiny stitches.

I bent my head low and brought my cheek to his garlicky knuckles. His skin was rough. I backed away, not awed but warmed by affection.

Someday, I'll get around to telling my husband. It'll start like this: You built a church because I failed to bear you a daughter. Consider this story her dowry.

MARY

Songs

This is the song: the Virgin and Jesus, the pantheon of saints, God our Father, incense, the somber knot of hair at the back of his head, grey-black beard, enormously wide blue eyes, equally enormous hands held in a motion of prayer: folded, neat.

Ever since he was ordained, our father no longer sits at the piano to play for us. In church, he chants notes that wrap around us and disappear like smoke. Or stay with us for days, melodies Joseph and I hum without thinking. His songs mourning Jesus' death are irresistible.

Is he turning saint, my own father?

And if I try to follow, where will we be going?

Soft Foods

I hold the spoon to Samuel's eager mouth. Feed him soft foods, mashed things. Sometimes he chokes, and I have to put a finger down his throat to hook whatever's blocking his windpipe.

I put a finger down my own throat after I've realized, too late, that food wasn't what I wanted inside me that day.

Mother always cooks.

GOODBYES

Since he became a priest, all our goodbyes are incomplete. He's a tired, pale, extraordinarily long face above a plate of greens.

But his blue eyes still dance.

When I was small, he was the sound of inept scales or brilliant arpeggios from the room next to the kitchen. Eating bread with olive oil and grated tomato, I listened.

Now, he's always gone before dawn.

CHOIR

Joseph has a startling deep voice with our father's perfect pitch. Samuel's high voice goes off course, lands in the vicinity of the angels, or the cats. Eleven years old, the two of them.

CALENDAR OF SAINTS

I was five when they were born.

This many years later, Samuel is still almost a baby. Joseph can be remote. Our father can be as well, but only when exhausted by chanting and lack of nourishment. There are several forty-day fasts in the calendar of saints.

SPINNING

How does a priest's mind differ from any other? Is it the words it uses to say things to itself or something else? A discrepancy in focus?

When I can't sleep at night, I imagine my father's mind working differently, sometimes almost not working at all—spinning without catching until it falls in a movement that holds it, spreading out to include eternity. Then the mind moves ahead to the next part of the Gospel, someone else's words.

I'm suspicious of anyone's words but my own.

FATHER

Closing up the church for the night, my father leaves the candles lit. One fallen candle and the whole place would go up in flames. But he won't deny the believers their prayers—in God's eye for the time it takes the candle to burn.

In the cobblestoned lane outside, there's mewling. At home, we nurse sick kittens with eyedroppers and rags.

AMETHYST

I despise my name not only because of the connotations, the expectations; I'm wise enough to suspect I'd hate any name that's mine.

At fourteen, I changed it from Mary to Amethyst, a name with no equivalent in the roster of saints. Some days, I've said: Mother, if you don't call me Amethyst, I won't eat a thing on that plate.

I've overturned china onto clean linen, the reds, the browns bleeding an auburn sun onto my mother's white tablecloth.

No one's ever called me Amethyst.

SAINT

I know I'm difficult. Who wants to be compared to a saint?

LICORICE CATS

When I was the boys' age, church was for christenings and Easter. Before our father became a priest, I'd spent enough time in churches to know the clingy scent, the humidity of human breath. I always kept a handful of licorice cats in my pocket to make the minutes pass.

MOTHER

My mother has become one of the neighborhood women with their heavy bags and aching feet, dark clothing and covered heads.

Has God entered this home? My father sings heavenly tunes that silence every other voice.

HOMEMADE VANILLA

Their first birthday? Grandma's homemade ice cream, the season's strawberries quartered over vanilla.

Now that I don't eat, I review the meals of my life.

FARMER'S MARKET

In the outdoor market, each piece of fruit has an aggressive attractiveness. Shiny apples in green, yellow, red. All the kinds of pear I've ever tasted. Winter strawberries, flown in from a warmer climate. Even mushrooms entice me with their immaculate shape, the hard roundness. I walk through, tasting with my eyes.

If I want to live, I need to eat. But having resisted the most delicious particulars of nutrition, I can't turn back.

I eat dry rusks so hard I know eventually they'll crack a tooth. A cracked tooth would make eating a more difficult chore.

I feed myself porridge, a food out of fairy tales.

It's hubris, I know, but I can't help feeling saintly as I walk starving, adoring through the stalls of fresh fruit and vegetables.

CATS

I put out a pan of milk and the fish bones saved from my father's meal. The cats purr and brush up against my legs, a dreamy touch. Sea creatures in water.

Animals can't decide not to eat; I delight in making myself more than animal.

It's so human to want.

BELIEF

He was a music teacher who went from house to house, making small children learn their scales. He'd put his faith in music until one morning he awakened to the church, a family spanning the ages.

Calendar, saints, prayers, incense. He's always needed to believe—I'm sure this is the belief he'll die with.

NAUGHTY GODS

One day that shelf was empty. They'd been his, relics from the days when he loved things ancient. Back then, he had no patience for any religion but the kind with fluctuating, naughty gods.

How did he give them up? Athena and Artemis. Zeus, Dionysus. Hermes. Demeter. Hera. Hephaestus. Where does he store them now? Are they still in his brain? Locked in a cell?

Do they ever sing to him, entreat him to let them free?

DESIRE

I hold desire in my body, maintain it by refusing to slake it.

Thirst and hunger, my food.

Is our family in tatters because he's taken on a godly life? Or because I've found God in hunger?

APPLES

It's so easy to resist a meal, chip off pieces of juicy apple and slip them in the side of my mouth. An apple a day.

I've taken to calling him "*Pater*," more his as a parishioner than as a daughter.

FRESCOES

He could walk into the frescoes on the church walls. With beard, hat, black robes, he'd fit right in. He'd levitate slightly and be in the scene on the wall. My father the Father.

He says he lost his humanism years ago but where does that leave us?

CANDLES

Without lit candles, a church is infinitely dark.

One bright Easter, my candle fell aslant. The flame caught on a woman's thick hair, went up like a small forest fire, raging orange amongst the black-coated women.

I can't remember what he said to woo me back.

Where will he be standing when it finally dawns on him that I'm half the girl I once was?

BAPTISM

God's love comes through him most astonishingly when he's performing the duty of baptism. His parishioners claim there's no fretful baby who hasn't been calmed by his voice. He makes it sweet, wraps the child in the syllables of God's love.

I told him: Dad, when you christen the babies, you look as if you're giving birth. He was startled. What I didn't say: Which children do you consider more your own?

OUR MOTHER

Our mother's a pack horse, carrying bags home through crowded, broken streets.

Samuel

Samuel puts his face against the kitten's striped belly in the darkness he's made of shirt, priest's hat, and his own closed eyes. He smells the kitten's fur, lets it tickle his nose. The tail is caressing his cheeks when our father, a man in black, retrieves him, feet first, then holds him up by the elbows. The kitten scampers.

"Haven't I told you not to do that?"

Samuel nuzzles against our father's beard like a cat.

Prayer

I imagine my father's concern for me makes him know doubt. In four a.m. darkness, he knocks on the door of prayer by intoning a single syllable. Is rushed in. Can't remember another time when prayer rushed through him like that, a fast wind. He, too, is a wind, his presence in the world a rush of air.

He comes back to himself, *praying*, no longer prayer itself, now that he's shut his mouth.

Monasticism

His mouth won't open. Not with the nuns or his congregation. With us, it's even worse. He seeks the Bishop in his home—coffee cups are laid out and Lenten cookies put on a plate. My father begs for a few days of retreat which are granted by the old Bishop, still keen-eyed at close to a century.

It's been more than a year of lackluster eating. My mother is at the end of her less-than-saintly tether. Upon his return, he says, he'll take me to the nuns.

Jesus

Will you take me with you? In your suitcase?

86

Or bring back a few bushels of light?

THE EXQUISITE FLAVOR OF NO TASTE

The absence of flavor does things to me. My tongue flies away, abandons my body.

For dazzling seconds, I'm the notes that make up the song.

BECOMING OURSELVES

I eat small baroque meals and await visions. Joseph hits the high notes *and* the low ones, as if aiming to capture the entire universe with his voice. Samuel dangles saliva into his hands, forming translucent webs. The area beneath my mother's eyes darkens. My father's hands, teeth, and beard seem to grow longer, thinner.

It's our mother who's the saddest, with nothing to hold her up but a disintegrating family. The web she once held between her hands is broken. All that's left—discrete globs of spit.

I'd be willing to wager that hungry, I hit more notes, including sharps, flats and even smaller divisions of sound—the sounds only animals can hear—than the genius Joseph with his immense sturdy voice that, at this moment between childhood and adolescence, covers the world.

The difference? No one can hear my notes but me. It's a song I swim in as I move, dizzy, fortified by hunger. Because hunger, too, is a song. Nothing like my father's chant. Even less like Joseph's all-encompassing sound. This song is harsher, all dissonances and morbid perfections.

It's not a question of weight. I don't care about any number but infinity: God's number.

Bringing me back once again, as always, to him.

87

KILLING THE HUSBAND

Sometimes you have to kill the husband as much as it kills you, too, to do so. This is a psychological death—he'll probably be watching soccer on t.v. as it happens. It's painless. He remains unaware, sorry only when his team loses. The death takes time, hours or even days, but, once enacted, you breathe freely, love him with more passion. He may never even know, rapt in his game, his imaginary wins and losses, the goals missed and scored.

MARRIAGE, A RECYCLING

In marriage one learns to make of even the most unfortunate-seeming events or emotions *something*.

Even bad sex: married, you don't always have the luxury of calling it so.

BOXED IN

It's calm today and almost sunny. But those tall bulky trees he's planted block the view of hills, sea, sky. He's boxed us in. Trees aren't always beautiful, I'm sorry.

MEDITATION

Each day is a strange meditation. A negotiable meditation? A meditation in fits and starts. A challenge, a boast, a conjecture, a slam.

POCKETS

Reaching into your pocket, you feel something warm and almost human, not quite slick. You think: We don't even *use* condoms anymore, and why would there be one in here, anyway? Anxious, you pull out a three-day old carnation, red, and folded in on itself. It still holds scent.

WINDLESSNESS

The quiet of a windless day: the world is huge but intimate. You feel you can call out to someone across the planet.

BREATHING

My husband came back from the doctor with a swollen hand. He'd gone for a check-up but the hand had intervened. The doctor wrote out a prescription for a cream and later made my husband exhale into a glass. It was a weak exhalation, and strangely so for a swimmer. Why are his breaths so shallow?

After raw cabbage doused in lemon juice, pepper, and sea salt, I sit in direct sun to think. Meanwhile, he's sleeping. By the time he's awake and knocking around in his heavy clogs, I've got it figured out.

"*You*," I tell him, "need to learn how to *breathe*. From the start. In and out. Slowly!"

He stands in front of me and breathes shallowly, into his chest.

"NO," I say, "breathe into your belly, the way babies do."

He says: "But I'm not a baby." Then turns and stomps off in his noisy clogs.

My vision is this: Slow deep breaths would cure his ills. Impatience and irritability. Wrinkles and rogue hairs! Low blood sugar. I know it would work, but I can't breathe for him.

Dead Bulbs

He's always letting light bulbs die. At night, we move around like readers of a different braille, our hands grabbing empty space.

Secrets

She felt as if her secrets kept popping out.

Photography

When it started raining (just before nine this morning), he went to get the camera. The sun was shining through the drops so there was actually something to capture, but still—taking pictures of the rain?

Clouds

These clouds, and my inability to do anything but mark their existence by using the word that refers to them—sunlit puffs, their bottoms grey.

Slow-dying

Have I poisoned the well? Do we sip water containing traces of poison?
Isn't it all a slow-dying anyway?
And if not slow, then fast.

Logic:

The necessity of giving up something forever.
The impossibility of doing so.

Shoes

My husband's shoes are so noisy they should be jailed.

He's angry with me for wearing my outside shoes in.

SELF-PORTRAIT?

Those crazy birds (a pair flying into the glass door, trying to get to the light)—is that us?

EASTER

Today, the Easter scent and the quiet of the spring day force themselves on our consciousness. And of course there's no getting around the roses, like dollops of frosting on the vines.

PERSPECTIVE

Nothing.
Or everything. Depends on how you look at it, and at what time, from what angle, through which drop of water.

HYSTERIA

How can I have said the things I said today?
What hysteria? What ridiculous desire to destroy?

He's everything to me.

My stomach.
My throat.

My weather.
My constant weather.

OVERLAP

His heart encompasses mine.
Our hands a circle.
My feet, his kidneys.
His eyes, my lips.

Chlorine and Liver

The house reeks of chlorine. She believes in it, like a god or a saint, and wraps us in the spell of it every other Sunday when she cleans. In the meantime, he's frying liver in the kitchen.

Chlorine and liver. Like some kind of curse.

Shyness

We have entirely peaceful hours by the fire, sitting opposite one another, reading. A peace that wells up into moments of love so strong you can only shy away from them.

Departure

I sent him on a treasure hunt of I love you's. He left one short note between my wallet and passport. When I found it, I cried.

She

So she was there with her husband, in the thick of winter, at last.

Distance

Sometimes even from across the street *or another room in the house*, the distance is piercing.

You

And then there's him, *you*—husband, lover, friend—*maker*.

ALL THE MEN

DOG

Before I moved into the house next door, he thought I would be the type of woman who would have a dog.

For weeks, he must have been excited by that expectation. But then, moving day came and it turned out I had no dog, cat, or child. So he, Jordan, became my dog and like a river, ran between the houses.

A little wild, somewhat rough, he knocks things over as if he had a tail. But it turns out that even if I don't have a dog, I'm used to that kind of wildness. Saying "never mind," I take him inside my lilac-and-green kitchen for frothy milk. I don't know yet to shout across the driveway to his mother: "Is milk okay?"

THAT THICK BLUE VEIN

Being dog comes naturally to him. Even cat wouldn't be hard. It's the other seducers that seem to confuse him: rat, lizard, sparrow. He pecks in the crook of my arm, the sensitive place where the vein shows blue and thick.

I'm reminded of others who've pecked at my veins, men I've known along the way:

A Ted

A saint takes on the contours of his time. People rush to listen to the storm that issues from his lips.

This is where I was: inside the house, doing the dishes.

Who has time for saints?

That Attraction

His saintliness, my barrenness: each a riff on saying no.

Engulfed by sameness, we split ourselves at the core. Two not very neat parts.

It's opposites that attract.

(That same Ted.)

Mid-Life

Never having thought of myself as shrink, healer, or shaman, certainly not mother, I know Jordan, the boy next door, sometimes thinks I'm a bird. *He* becomes dog whenever he comes near.

No men for a while now, but I have important relationships with my stuff. Cigarettes, car. The way I combine the two.

With needle and thread, glue and paint, I make things do what they seem to have not done before. But—epilepsy?

Could I lure him away from his malady?

Mid-life, half a century here with the rest of you.

Curiosity

I'm curious: Are there people who enjoy the fits? Could it ever be construed as interesting? Or always painful and terrifying (not to mention embarrassing)?

JORDAN

He gives me a sideways look, actually turning his head away from me then looking back, whenever he feels I'm about to say something dishonest or sentimental.

A SAMPSON, A DONALD

In the desert, he wore everything he owned to protect himself from the day's sun, the night's cold, eventually donning a toga—half-sheet, half-drapery—like a woman. Only his eyes were open on the world.

This is where he learned to see and be seen: in the sand-filled atmosphere, the scorching heat.

The desert: a place he returned to, in his heart if not with the soles of his feet. We used to go down to the dirty sand beach, pretending.

This period was long before he met me. I've never been to any desert but the internal one. The presence of men has prevented me from donning their clothing.

Two slits for my eyes.

These Donalds, these Sampsons.

SOUND'S COLOR

It takes too long to figure out: he hears color. That is: each color sounds.

The painting he makes in the living room (blue and orange paint on the rug, green on the wooden floorboards, sofa, his face, my arm) has a song to go with it. At first it's just noise but, heard repeatedly, I begin to get the hang of it. A jingle, it plays in my mind all night, threads itself through my dreams.

I wonder if he's singing it to himself at home in the house next door, waking himself up out of sleep with the force of his voice.

In the morning, I make coffee cake with blue-and-green frosting, trying to imagine the song it'll be: up-and-down, dancing around?

FIT

The world zooms in on him. Lights dance. Windows smash into "thousands of trillions of sparkles."

Is there anything in it to like? If he were cured, would he miss it?

DANIEL, DONALD, MICHAEL, STEPHEN, ANTHONY, JASON.

Seer? Healer? Saint?

Too many times, I thought: artist. But later learned: actor.

Leery now of shows of any kind.

QUESTION

How does a lie detector work?

MATH

How not to be the sum of their discordant parts? The bright heights they'd be better off not knowing. The darks they'd do anything not to dredge.

HERE, AGAIN

Deposited back on earth, the resumption of gravity is never without its shock. Here. Again. Oh. With a bark or a meow, a warm lick of the hand. This, I can take.

He licks it repeatedly, tongue warm as the milk he's just swallowed, wet on my smooth palm. He doesn't stop there. Bites my nails as if they're his own. I shoo him away.

Later, he finds me in another room, this one magenta, where I'm sewing old pieces into one. Thinking I've not seen him, he retreats, placing the screen door as silently as he can, then jumps the four wooden steps, springs across the thin rectangle of grass that divides the houses.

Bounds home.

HALF A CENTURY, REVISITED

Are there foods that can protect him? Words that push him over the edge? Thoughts? Has he ever dreamed a fit and awakened to find it was only a dream?

Cold shower? Hot bath? Blue jeans? Naked?

Are the conditions only internal? What about the weather—clouds, pelting rain, harsh sunlight? Snow?

And me? Half-a-century in the world and besotted with a wily five-year-old.

CLOSE-UP

That morning, he was making a mask with bits and pieces found on the kitchen floor: carrot top, button, cancelled stamps, mouse droppings. I screamed. He'd dropped to the floor, unable to stop his laughter. That's when I saw what epilepsy looked like close-up, but still from the outside.

EXCHANGE

We're all continually exchanging molecules, nothing being truly discrete.

Stephen, the One and Only

After each "game," his father left something for his mother—a piece of jewelry, bottle of perfume, a scarf. Or simply a fresh bill off his wad of cash.

Later, the woman took Stephen, her son, through her treasure chamber, a room at the end of the attic he and his brothers had never discovered in all their years of hide-and-seek. Had the wall absorbed the door to protect them? But it was there. He saw it. A museum of expensive belongings, crystal and scented, colored, heavy or light.

If I were you, he told me he'd told her, I'd have put a match to it all long ago.

But a person's feelings are so much more complicated than another can imagine.

Shame

Desire can be humiliating, especially after the heat of it wears off. Shame confines us to such narrow regions of desire. But cutting designs on your wife's skin as you take her?

Stephen said: "It's impossible, even at forty, to stop being a son, without a son of your own to make you a father."

This was our dilemma; I couldn't help him out of it.

Nothing: More Stephen

He said he wanted nothing but nothing, the purity of nothing, the clean air of emptiness. He coveted nothing the way he once died for certain obscure exhibits of the flesh: pouring over the flashy garter strap of a woman showing herself to a roomful of men.

He couldn't give up watching in the quiet cave of his mind (so he may as well have watched it in the flesh). In the end, he no longer touched any flesh but his own, when he had to, and that included (unfortunately) mine.

I understood that he had problems but I couldn't follow him toward the solution he'd devised.

Our Children (Stephen, Again)

The many children lost, months before their tiny lives were tenable. I still love him enough to believe the lost babies weren't his fault or mine.

Does he spend hours pursuing gloomy nothingness because he sees his children there? Do they smile at him from within the frail purity of his achieved state? (A state that toppled if the phone rang, a fly buzzed, or I walked carefully down the stairs, not ordinarily meaning to bother him.)

We left one another not cold but too sad for excitement: sadness bears little sensual fruit.

Shit (Paolo)

To himself he called it the shit. There were pictures that went along: finely detailed turds, curly and moist. Great pipelines of it, liquid and pungent. Shit surrounded him, infested him like something animal and alive.

I left quickly.

Future

Time, for him, breaks up. Like a telephone conversation interrupted by static or a lightning bolt.

Will he ever look back on these early days of fits as something rare and coveted, wanting again to be that boy driven from the ordinary by swirling lights and animal voices?

My Eyes

Walking through the bright scintillating scatomas that light (and obscure) my way. Is it anything like this?

Stephen's Dogs

Speaks with the lost babies, words that aren't exactly words, nothing he'd ever say to another human being.

Perhaps the dogs are recipients of these syllables, in a whispered rush, more caress than sense, but heartfelt.

Jordan, like a swift river,

destroys the plants I left on the bottom step of the porch, planning to work them into the soil the next morning. I'm certain he's the one who threw them randomly across my hardly fertile yard, blossoms torn from weak vines, clumped dirt bottoms up on ratty grass.

Surveying it from the kitchen window, coffee cup in hand, I think maybe he was right. Who wants to spend a Sunday digging around in wormy earth?

He arrives later, feigning distraction, his chirpy bright eyes darting around the need to pretend. I offer him foamy milk, add a drop of whisky for early morning solace.

So continues his life with women, mine with men.

ADAM AND EVA

HIS NEIGHBORHOOD

Adam's walls: an awkward grid of paper, canvas, shreds of fabric, rag. Viewed left to right, they narrate a difficult work, a discombobulation, a fork in the road, a murky kiss.

He lives there, heats food on a sterno, knows this is a worse sort of wilderness than any he's ever seen in nature—it's the kind that takes away everything you have, reminds you of things you've always wanted. For a year, there was a striped kitten, grey-and-black, that shared his food and brought in fleas.

When the kitten deserted, Adam hung posters on every telephone pole in the neighborhood.

The grande dame Eva—is she fan or player? Or just an old mother like his own, with dyed hair and unhappy feet?

She brought him a calico to replace the lost kitten. A woman who spent sixty years in a mansion. Now, like Adam, she roams and squats. Paints and culls. Occasionally destroys.

This part of the city is being turned dump to high-rise. He goes places, to see what he can find.

Alone behind his walls near the ballpark, he always knows when the home team is winning.

DREAM

In the dream, he dribbled a baby's head up and down the court, too nervous to shoot. The next day, he swears, he found a real baby on the dump heap, the only thing worth taking.

Adam holds the squirmy baby on his lap, an arm across its chest as if it's a toy or a football, something to keep near his heart. The baby twists enough to regard him, brings up a tiny hand to touch Adam's face. The moving fingers are like worms.

How will he get the baby up the ladder and over the wall?

"Baby, what's your name?" No tag, no sign. "I don't even know if you're a boy or a girl."

The baby likes his face, especially the hard knob of nose. Adam clowns his eyebrows up and down, opens his eyes wide, sticks out his tongue until the baby grabs it. When he pulls away, the baby's mouth opens. Tongue thrusts a little.

Is this a dream? Someone else's day?

"Copy cat, sloppy mop, jungle gym, born in sin. How'd you get here, baby?"

"Baby, show me your teeth." He shows his own, very white against his always-ruddy skin, and the baby obliges. It has four.

He carries the bundle across shards of glass, broken bedsprings, torn condom wrappers, twigs, certain the baby is real, but wondering if this is his life or someone else's.

CONVERSATION

His drawings go up and down the walls, a mural of sketches and paint on canvas, splodges and stories he's been trying to tell for years.

The baby's heavy. The head turns right, left, north, south.

He looks in the baby's face: "Baby, do you get it?" Leaves the bundle on a piece of dirty sheepskin and scrapes spaghetti from the pan.

Gurgling, the baby sounds like a bum pipe or a faulty motor. Then, plain crying.

"Hey, baby, hey Charlie, chill! I'll paint you onto canvas and then you'll be forever." But the baby isn't listening, can't understand.

OLDER WOMAN

Eva is old enough to be his mother or even his grandmother. Eva gave up the elegance of her former life for the paintings that refused to show up on canvas in a well-lit studio.

Adam watches as, from a sitting position, the baby leans over and props itself on all fours. Like a dog, or a baby, it crawls fast, away from the sheepskin square. It goes up to the wall with the Cat-in-the-Hat drawings and slaps the largest Cat with a pudgy palm, makes aggressive throaty sounds.

He thinks he's holding a phone; he thinks it's her voice coming through the receiver. The baby's clear eyes make him feel like crying. He hopes she gets there soon.

CAPELLINI

The baby pulls itself around on fists, elbows, and knees. Adam crouches low, spider-like, gangly, stares, makes funny faces. "Boo!" The baby laughs.

Then a smell comes from the baby; it paints a dark trail across the empty floor.

He tests the capellini against his wrist then holds a piece aloft, just above the baby's mouth. Curved and red, waiting.

Mostly toothless, the baby swallows the spaghetti with little gulping sounds, as if it's drinking milk.

On His Walls

Road Runner.
Donald Duck.
His toothless great-grandmother.
Someone's bashed-up Gibson.
Uma Thurman, whose hand he once touched.
Helium balloons with whole conversations written in tiny print he
can pen only when perfectly sober.
The conversation about marriage. The one about Jesus.
Nike swish.
Glow-in-the-dark Lego castle.
Christmas lights, drawn onto the window frame.
Biggie Smalls.

Flipping Words

"Humble baby, grumble baby, baby say your prayers. Crumble baby,
tumble baby. Sit up, let's rumble, baby."

"Ka-ka-ka-ka," it says, like a crow or a machine gun, blowing bubbles
at the back of its throat.

Making Beauty

Eva arrives, climbs the ladder with his hands open behind her in case
she stumbles.

Not more than a hundred pounds, the world contrasts sharply with
the blue in her eyes.

He notices again the little red ridges behind her ears where she once
let a surgeon use a knife on her face. Is it something he could do, with
his fine-motor hands, the fingers that can write whole conversations
inside the balloons above his cartoon characters' heads?

He promises himself that he'll never take a knife to a human face,
certainly not in an effort to make it more beautiful. Less beautiful,
yes. He could do that. Anyone can mar beauty.

But who can make it? The baby, in a corner, is growling, half-dog.

Her Teeth

Her teeth are older than her face. Disconcerting. Eva paints in chalk on broken sidewalks; when she walks through garbage, she keeps her head high.

Diapers

He nudges the baby onto its back, holds it there with a gallery of faces like a shuffled deck of cards.

The diaper is so heavy Adam wonders how the baby carried it around. He removes it, wraps a towel there. The tenderness of the baby's skin makes him flinch. On his rough hands, spattered paint like a tattoo. Once, he was a baby with tender skin, touched by warm hands.

Eva gives the baby a bottle. Then, like a father, he takes the sleeping baby, puts him on the floor beneath the largest of the Cats-in-the-Hat.

Outside, they hear the roar. The home team's winning. Beyond the stadium is deep black water all the way to China. It's a blackness he feels familiar with, one he's never succeeded in painting.

Now that the baby's asleep, he comes back to her with brushes and a palette. She laughs, knowing there's not another thing she can do.

She lets him paint the lines back onto her skin. Laugh lines holding her mouth. Worry between her eyes.

His own skin is crinkled, almost baked. Hardly old. Still, he's no infant.

Alive

With a finger, he traces the lines surgery removed. Then, with the finest paintbrush, he paints a scene on her straight pale back, in a blue-grey not unlike the color of her eyes. Trees, a brook, water gurgling over flat stones. He bends, drinks cool water.

He knows from her breath: everything she's forgotten comes back to her, immediate as lightning. She knows, and knows, and knows a thing so hard to grasp that each time she does, in a cluster of flashes, it's followed by darkness as thick and deep as the ocean.

She's never had more to lose; she's never been able to give up anything with more grace.

Pre-Columbian masks, first editions, originals. Photographs, coins, shells, costumes. Silverware, plates, fabric, furniture. Bookshelves, carved wood. Husband. Children. Their children. Everything gone, down to the mud beneath the foundations.

He touches her ears behind the lobe where the surgeon tucked the extra skin. Would like to loosen it by gnawing gently but keeps his even white teeth beneath raindrop lips.

He gives without asking for anything in return but it doesn't seem like charity.

HUNGER

When he turns back, Eva is gathering her shawls. Then, she's up the wall and out. The baby is gone.

He can't help thinking of what's delicious: Eva's shapes turned fruit—pear, apple, pomegranate. Compote. He misses the baby: its cries, its chubby limbs.

Adam paints everything over, stealing from himself. Forgetting and celebrating. He puts the baby there: fat forearms and tiny fingers. It's the first time he's painted something that's drawn his own tears.

Finished, he climbs the wall, walks the streets, paints an intricate tag. His new moniker? A set of flying teeth that'll move across the universe finding the very best things to eat.

GRACE

GRACE'S MARK

A week after my family moved into a house directly across the street from Grace's, the two of us found ourselves sharing a formica-topped desk.

The first day of seventh grade, she'd been adamant that I sit on the right side. Of course I understood that it was because of the mark.

Half-way into the semester, in the middle of a math quiz, Grace pulled her blouse up over her face and said: "All right, everyone. Forget the face and talk to me now."

RAGING COUNTRY

When you see the mark that's shaped like a raging country on the left side of her face, you experience a disturbing mixture of disgust and fascination. Eventually, you forget about it.

But there were children who wouldn't let her forget. Scar-face. Monkey-face. Adults either went out of their way to be sympathetic or couldn't hide the two-pronged mixture of emotion. As children, we knew exactly which teachers felt what—about Grace's mark as well as Kelvin's dark skin.

Children are cruel. I might have liked to be cruel to her myself, but couldn't: we became quick friends. Even as a twelve-year-old, she'd visited places the rest of us had never been.

Now, after years of knowing Grace, sometimes it's as if I'm seeing her for the first time. I become fascinated all over again. She has a normal quite pretty face rendered unusual by the mark. Really, it's only a (slightly raised) different color of skin. Now, though, the fascination is only tenuously connected with the mark: she's been around.

Her First Map

Grace had a map not on her wall the way some children do, but on her ceiling. She said it was complicated to pin it up there, but her father had done it using the longest of the long ladders from the basement.

I've always pictured that it was newly present when she came back from school one afternoon: tidy, flat against the ceiling, imperious. Sleeping on her back, she faced the entire world.

Between the Houses

At thirteen years old, Grace had spinster-like qualities. She refused to stay in a room without circulating air and was always slamming open the windows of that old house. I put up with her; the quirks were entertaining.

Outside her own room, electric street lights hummed in the cool air. Right across, two stories above the passing cars, I could see my own house, small and self-contained. I felt sorry for it and turned away quickly, glad to be in Grace's huge cold room.

The house was so large that her mother used one telephone line to call the children on the other line to dinner. Grace's mother was rarely aware of the fact that we'd often come from roast beef and potatoes or spaghetti and meatballs at my house. Years later, she laughed when we thought to tell her of our many double-dinner nights.

At Grace's house we ate flank steak, cooked on the outside, raw in the middle. Her younger sister licked cream cheese from a knife, and wouldn't speak to us. Jealousy hung in the halls of their house like the scent of a new perfume. Marci always thought I should have been her friend rather than Grace's. Her face was empty of marks, pure and plain.

After eating uncountable slices of flank steak, we spooned coffee and mint chip ice cream straight from the carton. I thought it made us family.

Later, Grace and I retreated to the telephone room, a small cubicle papered in thin red-and-white stripes. It looked peppermint but smelled lavender. We got out the book. She sat on the telephone room stool, covered in red velvet like a pin cushion. I took the leather-covered phone book from the shelf and let her choose. She opened to a white page, I closed my eyes and lowered my finger to a particular name. Most people hung up once they figured out that we were two bored girls looking for some excitement.

On bad days, we called Ben Woo. 885-2204. He kept us on the phone, asking where we lived, why we didn't have something else to do, what we looked like. He was an old Chinese man who lived way downtown. I pictured a bald head, the slittiest of slitty eyes, and a gray Fu Manchu beard all the way down to his penis.

We didn't know that Marci stood silently outside the door of the telephone room while we placed our calls. One Saturday morning we were called into the kitchen. Light came in through the picture window that let in the Bridge and the Bay.

Grace's mother was severe. "If someone traces those calls, the police will take us to jail. Not you. You're minors. Then what?" We suffered a long moment of silence.

"No more crank calls. Understood?" She included me in the severity of her gaze; I understood it as a kind of adoption.

Afterwards, I slunk back to my own smaller house across the street. Sometimes it was a relief to leave the vast expanses of theirs, knowing, of course, how easy it would be to gain entrance once again.

BACKGAMMON

Many years later, Grace wrote to me saying that she'd always thought my life looked interesting—she wanted to visit. A couple of weeks passed before she took several planes, a boat, and two cars to take a closer look.

By the time she arrived here, she'd realized a few things about her life. I was someone she'd known almost always, a person she could measure herself against.

We played backgammon together on the terrace, looking out on the olive trees. I beat her every single time and didn't once think of letting her win.

As the sky darkened, we poured red wine and dug pistachios out of their shells, pressing plastic against the wooden board. Eventually we left the pieces as they were—that's when we began to talk.

INTERVIEW

I'm still not sure whether she placed me in the position of an interviewer, encouraging me to ask questions she wanted to answer, or if it just happened that way. We said a great many things during her stay but while she had come, ostensibly, to see my life, I think she told me more about hers than I told her about mine.

I live in two countries. I'm married. Our children are grown and studying far away.

DOGS

She said: "My mother loves the dog more than she loves me."
I said: "Grace, you're forty and you can say such a thing?"
"But it's true," she said.
And I had to stop and think about dogs.

They come when they're called.

They let you touch them and, if you don't, they tend to put their cold nose against your warm hand.

CLEAN SHEETS

One evening we went out together to the café by the sea. Before we'd had a drink, she seemed so much the person she had been at thirteen. But with her glass of wine and my scotch, everything changed.

She did most of the talking and I listened, trying to follow along and at least have some idea of where each story took place. She'd been to thirty times as many places as I have. After a while, Mozambique seemed to merge with Zimbabwe and Rwanda and eventually Kosovo and back around to Guatemala.

Talking with her was a little like actual travelling. It could be thrilling, but after a while the thrill leaked away and you wanted simply to climb into your own bed with a clean set of sheets.

BIRTH MARKS

Some people with those birthmarks are beautiful. The mark, the red land of it leaves a scintillating choice for the viewer: beauty or ugliness? But Grace wasn't beautiful enough on the one side to offer such a split. Her face was pretty in a useful way, but hardly kind.

Her body was graceful and lithe, if very small.

FOUR MEN

One night she slept with four men, one after the other, in the light of a fire fed with scraggly brush. She couldn't say whether she did it for lust or pleasure, fear or curiosity. She said it bothered her, occasionally, not knowing.

PORN

I didn't want to picture certain things.

During the entire conversation I was aware of my brow, so furled I must have forged new lines. I couldn't unfurl it, couldn't say anything. Just meaningless exclamations. And at certain points I covered my face with my hands and rubbed my eyes, as if I were watching something taxing. I was.

I didn't want to see her naked.

She said she'd come to watch me in my life but as much as she may have wanted to catch a glimpse of mine, she was aching to show me what she had done with hers, how she had put in the years, what she had acquired and lost along the way.

I realized that she'd lost things I'd never dreamed of having.

INFORMATION

"When people are attacked with long knives, machetes, it's particularly brutal and personal. You wouldn't want to do that to people you didn't already feel close to."

I noticed that she'd picked up things along the way. Information.

She mentioned things in a matter-of-fact tone. I wasn't sure if it was pure performance or the attempt to say something impossible.

GRACE, THROUGH THEIR EYES

The day we were invited to eat at the neighbors', she brought out her camera just as the meal was being served: plates of braised goat, homegrown broccoli, cucumber and tomato salads from their garden. She liked the look of Old Kosti's hands, black from picking walnuts two days before.

The family presented all their best dishes including, of course, the roasted goat's head. They split the skull and spooned out the greyish-pink brain, adding lemon. Grace had eaten brains before. She put some on her fork and ate it almost daintily. As she wiped her lips with a paper napkin, Old Kosti handed her one of the eyeballs, a cloudy bulb, pronged onto a tin fork. I looked away from her. I didn't want to see her humiliated.

It was a windy day. My hair slapped me in the face as I watched her success register in Agapi's raised black eyebrows and Arhontoula's more restrained look of surprise. It made Grace something more than a mere visitor.

When I see them, one or the other still asks me about my friend "with the spot on her cheek."

FEARLESS TERRITORIES

She carried a small-scale version of the map that had looked down on her from the ceiling of her childhood bedroom. Certain parts were infested with dots of red or blue, yellow, green. I had no idea what the colors stood for.

When I asked, she laughed and said: "Hey, try to guess."

HAPPY MISERY

Grace makes you aware of her misery without elucidating the reasons. You could call it a happy misery.

PEACOCKS

One afternoon we stood against the fence for close to an hour watching the peacock in the field below the house, waiting for him to open his feathers.

Early on, she said, she decided that she didn't want a husband. Whenever mine was around, she became irritable: she'd never been good at sharing.

The peacock performed only once we started walking back up to the house. In the late afternoon light, the blues and greens were dazzling.

Sometimes almost anything can make you feel pity. Sometimes you're just ripe for it.

Lively Conversations

She'd always been interested in pursuing medicine. She wanted to see inside a human being.

We had lively conversations about my children's various surgeries but she started talking about her new camera when I brought up the subject of their births.

Camera

Grace collected bones along with feathers, paint swatches, old computers and boxed children's games until she came into the possession of a digital camera. Then, she stopped collecting things, put everything in storage, and took pictures. It seemed benign and ecological, everything contained in a file on her computer.

Killing

The closest she'd come to killing was a killer: S., a mercenary in Angola, boyfriend of two weeks. "Paradoxically, he was a particularly gentle lover," she said. "All tongue and fingertips. I was pleasantly shocked."

Wrinkles

Grace wasn't interested in simple answers. For instance, she'd never been to a spa. She wasn't curious about botox or other treatments. She'd had surgeries that accomplished nothing but a slight tucking of the country on the side of her face. "Like wrinkling a sheet of paper," she said.

I touched my own when she said it, with both hands.

Wallpaper

She told me she once slept with a man made of tattoos. "Slept with, didn't fuck. I spent the night examining the various designs on his skin. Not overly conducive to sexual rapture, to be perfectly honest. Fascinating wallpaper though," she said, and chuckled.

SURGERY

It takes fucking a doctor to make her understand that she's always wanted to be a surgeon. He let her into the OR—scrubbed, booted, masked.

Watching the appendectomy was more exciting than sex. Or so she'd thought at the time.

When she talked about knives, I thought it was because she wanted to cut off the mark. But maybe it wasn't that at all. Maybe she wanted to use them to pierce through skin, to get a glimpse of what was underneath.

LIMITATIONS

As young boys, my children performed small surgeries on living beings: ants, grasshoppers and beetles. They even buried a kitten alive, not quite aware that what they were doing would kill it. I didn't need to punish them: they suffered when they realized the limitations of a life.

Grace knew no limitations. More than mere appetite, she had a startling greed.

Like newlyweds in the parental home, my husband and I didn't turn to each other once for the duration of her stay. She ate from the pan of meat with her fingers, called out to me in the darkness after we'd already said goodnight.

My husband insisted that she hadn't been properly weaned.

LEADER

The light shone off him. One of the soldiers lifted her up to see— she was tiny—and from there, against a darkening blue sky she saw him, their leader. Whether it was a trick of the light or something that coursed through his blood, she couldn't say. But the thing is, *he shone.*

She said she'd never been in the presence of a man like that.

Grace's Brother

She didn't believe in heaven or hell but knew that her little brother, the one who'd died before he ever went to school, had to be somewhere. She still felt him, sometimes, and mostly in places he'd never been. It wasn't that she didn't know she carried him with her, but the way she happened upon him—in Sri Lanka or Mozambique—was so elegant and real. She couldn't *not* say it was him.

Thirty years later, she remembered him as the only person who'd ever looked at her without flinching. She seemed close to tears when she told me. Even the intimation of tears in her voice brought them up quickly in me. But she didn't cry.

The Dogs That Barked All Night

"In the blistering African heat whenever I'd sink into sleep, the dogs roused me from it. Eventually one of the drivers fucked me to oblivion. After that, the dogs' noise didn't bother me."

Toby's Mother

"I'd been away from there for a while, maybe three years, and when I returned, they knew me as Toby's mother. Eventually I went back for a third time, maybe another trip two or three years later and they called me Paddy's grandmother. Dogs reproduce quickly, compared to humans."

ADRENALINE

The morning of her departure, we were rounding up escaped rabbits. They'd dug a huge hole beneath their large hutch and kept appearing at different spots along the hill above the house. We were frantic, trying to herd them back inside.

At the bus stop just before she hoisted herself, with her heavy knapsack, onto the first step of the bus she said: "I guess I have a high level of tolerance for adrenaline. Unless there's a rush of it, I can't feel a thing."

LETTER

Grace wrote that while she was here, it was as if we'd gone back in time to when we were teenagers living across the street from one another. That's how it is with old friends. But she moves around so quickly there's no sense of gathering anything to her.

In the letter, she asked: "Is my life an extravagant spending or a miserly frugality? Write when you can. Love always."

RICHARD

A year or so later, we're both visiting our mothers, who still live on opposite sides of that street.

"After being face-to-face with a monkey," Grace says, "I feel more sympathy for these dogs." She comes close and whispers, "I'm sure my mother loves them more than she loves me."

Grace calls every one of them "Richard."

Richard, the favorite Richard, sits quizzical when Grace comes round her mother's kitchen. "You know that look dogs get—almost arch and yet more curious than anything? A little hurt? When he does this, I know Richard is thinking, 'Why does this woman have a face like a monkey's ass?'"

She laughs and I watch her swat at Richard as he swipes past her, tail high and ranging.

A week later, she pays an artist to tattoo a Richard on her left shoulder. She tells me: "I figure that when I'm alone in some far-off land, I can lift my sleeve and lean against it. In El Salvador, Italy, Russia, and Mexico, I've watched people praying to icons. This Richard is the closest I can possibly get."

HIS MOTHER'S CATS

STUDENT

Almost six-feet-tall and lithe, Oedipus couldn't read, couldn't study, had difficulty doing anything he was supposed to do. He was a student whose mind had deserted him.

Text before him, he stared beyond the purple-stained shutters at wisteria vines bare of flowers. The words were smooth on the page, a smoothness he tested again and again with the tip of his index finger, letting the other long fingers join in.

A government-issued textbook, it would be torn into small pieces as soon as he'd taken the exam in June.

For hours, he sat at the desk, the length of him bent mid-spine under the burden of ennui and habit, a pencil between his fingers making random marks in the air.

CATS SWARM

In his house, cats swarm. He can't move without cats dodging his feet or jumping toward them, his feet like large mice.

"Their breath stinks; how can I bring someone here?"

"The cats eat the flies," she says. His mother's painted purple toes stick out of purple string sandals.

He wants to smoke but doesn't have any cigarettes. Walks to the kiosk, buys a new Asterix and a pack of Marlboros.

119

At home, she makes him an omelette. He eats half of it and pushes the rest onto the floor. Cats pounce.

When his father finally comes back, the house goes dark. He stays up waiting to hear their noise but it never comes.

SMOKING

Mother cats give birth to babies on the bathroom floor, in the kitchen beneath the oven or a bloody wet mess on his pillow. Kittens crawl against him all night long, not exactly waking him up, but there, breathing at his knees or stuck in an armpit through the night.

When his father's gone for good, Oedipus realizes two things: a mother isn't a wife, and his is crazy. The house stinks of cat. He douses himself in aftershave from a blue bottle.

"Ma, we need to get rid of them." She smirks; he lights a cigarette with a white Bic.

"Smoking and cats are not the same thing." She says it slowly, wisely, the way she often speaks now that his father, her husband, is gone.

For a week, he smokes in his room, leisurely, with the window cracked, stroking the gray male, the only one he can stand, the one he's known his whole life.

SUMMER

He'd always liked summer best.

It was summer when the cat ran into the narrow tree-lined street outside their purple-trimmed house and a car slammed into its sleek gray head.

He didn't see it, only heard from others that it was red and shiny, a car he might have liked to own some day. He imagined that the owner, someone like himself, would have been sorry to know he'd hit a cat that held together a boy's world.

He held the cat in both arms against his chest. One move and the cat—mangled, maimed—would be gone, off the table, across the slippery linoleum, and back out into the early morning traffic. He watched the needle go beyond fur, felt it catch against flesh, the slight jump, and then the drug worked very quickly on the small body. The elasticity left it. Limp, small and shrunken, just a curve of warm, dampish fur. He put it down on the table and it stayed. Like a hand-muff or something a woman would put against her throat for warmth. Death hadn't come; life had gone and there was no urging it back. His once-lively cat was useless, a thing.

He took the cat home in a beach towel, buried the furry body (heavier than before but also smaller) beneath a pomegranate tree. Hoped it would bear fruit. Promised himself that if it did, he'd eat the bitter seeds.

Running

He no longer smoked—a cigarette in his hand made him miss the feel of pulse and fur.

He ran with the dog through back alleys, around the tipping minaret to the harbor.

He missed his father, would have done anything to see him coming around the corner. But he had the dog: she took him places he'd never been.

Curtains

Oedipus liked it when the dog ran down the alley to a building on the street parallel to theirs. When the woman was home, gauzy white curtains billowed from the window. He passed slowly, knowing his dog was with the other one.

Sometimes he could see her moving behind the curtains; he heard her talking to someone he couldn't see.

He waited for the high-pitched howl that let him know the dogs were stuck. You were supposed to scare the dogs apart but he preferred to stand nearby and inspect. Maybe he would be a scientist. Or a vet. A journalist. Or a simple playboy.

FLUTES

His father's manic flute made fragile things tremble and eventually crack. Why did she consent to share her bed with him?

He arrived, flute in its case, dark hair receding rapidly. Each weekend he looked different—almost as if he weren't Oedipus' father but someone else, his mother's new boyfriend. It was sick when they sat down together at the table, set with bamboo placemats that gathered crumbs between the sticks, and ate a hearty meal. Oedipus and his father talked soccer scores while she, the mother but no longer the wife, stirred something to completion on the stove. Everyone ate with vigor.

GYPSIES

He followed the dog through the streets, spied on what he thought were prostitutes in pink-colored buildings by the harbor. He walked past the gypsy camp before and after school. Stole money from his mother to buy a louder alarm clock, and left the house on weekdays before she was awake. Weekends, he passed through the market where farmers sold brighter-looking fruit and vegetables at lower prices than the ones in town. There were gypsies too, seated behind high piles of women's underwear, small mountains of cotton and nylon in every color. He liked the gold teeth and shining black eyes, found their beautiful women more beautiful than others.

They said gypsies stole blond babies. He wasn't a baby but his hair, even at fifteen, was still blond.

Dogs' Tails

He thought about the way dogs' tails traced shapes in the air.

Wind Instruments

He allowed his hand to do the thing to himself but only on the days when the dogs stuck. That was rare; he was crazy with the need to do it every single day. Some days it reached his chest, cut off his breathing, made his heart pitch a scattered beat.

Once, while watching the stuck dogs, his eyes stopped functioning properly. He felt blind.

His father drifted through the house without warning, drifted out again. Just a wind.

He heard the scruffy romping fury of the neighborhood dogs from a mile away.

His mother in her bed alone: purple bed, purple toenails, cold purple feet.

At the movies, they sat on opposite sides. He didn't want her to see him watching the movie and, for that matter, he didn't want to watch her watching it.

Why was one of the dogs always like that, the perfect tube of glistening red out in the air?

Weight

"Even when I eat this much," (his mother showed him with thumb and forefinger) "I gain rather than lose."

"Are you pregnant?"

"If I am," she said, "the baby inside me is ten years old."

He tried not to show his shock.

SMELL

His sense of smell became so powerful that he could hardly live in the house: everywhere, the smell of shit.

Oedipus stopped eating her food. Lived on saltines and chocolate wafers for a week. He knew he should have been building up his muscles but he liked giving up something, didn't mind being less.

MUMMIES

Their bodies side by side? Like mummies?

BLIND

He wanted what they had, but knew he'd never be a dog.

The neighborhood dogs came in the afternoon. Some part of the sun's light reached him through the blindness. The dogs surrounded him and took him down.

The heady draw of nicotine was a past life.

EATING

After running with the dogs, he smelled it on himself. Sitting at the table, he located the food with his hands, his mouth. The odor of his canine body filled his nose. Ashamed, he ate wildly, using his fingers, then licked the plate to a smooth perfection. By then, he was mostly dog.

BLOOD

He followed them like a tail for days, until they were following him.

Regular as the sea, the swish of his blood kept him in one place, the cats circling. Blood, the only sound worth listening to. But the price of sound was a diminishment of scent. He ate whatever she put on the table, finding it with his hands, bringing it to his face.

His mother thought it was the gray cat, which she'd let out by mistake. Blaming herself, the way mothers do.

The only thing he missed: shooting baskets with a new, pumped-up ball. The satisfaction of hand-to-eye.

How

He knew why it had happened, but not how. Only knowing how would reverse the spell.

He ate with his hands or a spoon. Spilling, he heard the displeasure in her breath. She walked him to school, picked him up, read his lessons to him all afternoon and into the evening. The cats circled, the t.v. stayed off until, exhausted by another sightless day, he found his way to bed. He heard her in the other room, t.v. low but not as low as it had been the week before. She was beginning to break.

Visions

In the dark behind his eyes, he saw pictures. Movies flowed. People he'd never met kaleidoscoped into his mother's purple house, the neighboring church with its gold dome, the blue-and-white school across the street. He rode a bicycle in and out amongst the children, played basketball on a black-top unmarked court. He visited the gypsies in their encampment and the women in their pink house.

Things were released in him, away from the light. He talked its electricity in school—and heard the click of silence before their nervous laughter.

His mother tried to coax him from the dark with piles of fried potatoes under a handful of melting cheese, mussels, a steak he picked up in his hands.

Cats walked the grape trellis to the high kitchen window, jumped past the sink to land on the table. His mother's shouting brought him back to himself, seated on a chair, grease running down his face.

His father's voice was arrogant, arranged: "So you think you want to be a vet?"

HEARING HIS MOTHER'S HEART

She roamed the house in the dead of night, moved by touch, cats brushing against her naked ankles. With no husband, she shut the house against the night, held in the darkness.

One night, Oedipus tricked her, turning on the small lamp beside his bed. He heard the pause of her slipper-shod step on bare marble. Then he heard her heart move faster in hope, until she got the joke and returned to her room, her narrow bed. Even when his father was in town, he never heard anything but sleep coming from there.

She touched him: hair, shoulders, hands, calves. Smoothed his eyebrows, fingered his cuticles, his nails. Steered clear of certain parts that, for the absence of touch, seemed dark. Only the dogs and the ladies in the pink house attended to those parts of him.

Sated with motherly fingers, his brows, cheeks, the backs of his hands were colorful.

He thought the blindness would abandon him if she would loosen herself from the house, walk into the street and find someone. "The world is full of people," he wanted to say. "It must be so easy to match the lit-up parts. Aren't we all the same?"

She'd abandoned herself. In the dark, her parts didn't shine. He had to find a girl his height, his age—a pretty girl with blond hair and breasts just right for his hands. Everything would go out of the world when he opened his eyes on the girl. The darkness would pour away.

MOTHER AND SON

They lived together in a three-room house, chaste mother and periodically blind son, cats streaming in a smelly wave until the afternoon she came home lugging four gallons of milk and the news that a man several houses up the road had chopped off his mother's head and boiled it in an iron pot.

He gave up on the dogs, the gypsies, the ladies in the pink house, including the fat motherly madam who insisted on testing the firmness of his penis each time he went through the misty red-tinted light he couldn't see but somehow comprehended. His eyesight improved overnight.

Sundering Twins

She knows the girls at school won't believe it because it's *her*, the ungainly twin, the unbeautiful, dull twin. No one says it aloud but she knows the intuition people share is that the *other* twin, the one with hair she can sit on, jutting bones, and clear skin somehow absorbed more of the energy, the goodness, the stuff—whatever it was—when the sperm did its job and the cells began dividing.

Always part of, never exactly one, she went her own way dreamily, nervously, watched people from the high windows of buildings, eavesdropping, something of a collector.

He was someone who arrived almost whenever she wanted him to—and that was rarely.

This was a girl in a family in a building not too far from the park. A girl with a collection of bags containing things she didn't want to give away. Rocks, old candy, lipstick, shells.

Her twin was tall; her twin was sane; her twin was bigger-than-life, two-in-one. She'd sucked up more amniotic fluid and come out better, grandiose.

These were the secret thoughts this twin, the smaller, only-half-made twin thought to herself over breakfast—breakfast that was also lunch and dinner—the day that it happened.

He was alone, an only child who presented himself as an orphan. He liked to say that, she could tell, and now she allowed herself a slight sardonic upturning of her lips, rather than the aghast and sorrowful look she didn't know better than to offer the first time he'd said it.

So he was an orphan and she was the lesser half of a pair.

He: is of medium height and skinny, but he's trying to do something about it. He won't show you until he knows you *well*, the way he sometimes feels that he knows her, the tattoo circling his bony ankle. It's a rainbow of colors—blue, red, green, black—with no meaning beyond its there-ness: a fact on his skin, a circle, a meeting on the other side. And the colors—he's always liked colors.

Whereas she likes weight.

And holds more of it against her bones than she probably should. Her mother calls it padding; she knows it's soft armor.

The clunk and plink of her collections, the nails high on her closet walls, holding things she can't.

Above the nails, a window onto the heavens.

They are not for one another and yet they are: they sidle across the schoolyard then seem flung together like magnets.

She sneaks him into the building, past the doorman and the maid, her mother, and her twin. In the closet, together, they look out the window onto sky and buildings, and a short piece of street. Behind them, on nails, is her stuff. She could take down the bags, one by one, and relinquish her hold. Or strengthen it.

The boy is thin and pocky. If he doesn't touch her, she'll touch him, then they'll burst through the small rectangle of window in her closet and fly between the chimneys.

They look out onto a mostly blank sky. Of course it depends on how they position themselves. If one would stand on the other's back, he or she could see parts of the roofs of surrounding buildings. She fantasizes that they can see the park. But neither will offer his back to the other: they're standing close, without touching.

How can they be like this, she thinks, and still nothing? Maybe it's because he's too thin, she's too fat. Opposites attract, don't they? Not always, she avers.

Curiosity nabs her: she lunges. Tastes newly grown mustache and sweaty skin. Gags a little.

She says: Is this how you do it?

He is un-resistant, worm to bone. The stuff in her hand wiped off on the red corduroy bag filled with ticket stubs and empty lipstick cases.

She is sodden, heavier than ever with the knowledge that he's capable of giving in a way that merely leaves stuff on her hand.

Next time she'll try her mouth.

She thinks maybe it's girls she likes and isn't ashamed until she thinks of some of the ones at school and what they would say if they knew. Then realizes they already do. They must. Which is why her life is the way it is, solitary and booming, jagged, a stutter.

Next time, she reels him in with a lock of just-goldened hair—she keeps it longish for appearances but would prefer it shorn—to look at all the useless things she collects. They've already been in the closet and nothing really happened. This time could be different. She's aiming to collapse two bags into one, the rocks and the coins, just to show him how similar any two sets of things really are. Or different.

The boy is reed-thin, his face is angled planes. He watches her through glasses and winces when she tells him to take them off.

"Why?"

"Because I can't see through them."

"You're not supposed to; I am."

She finds it easy to be mean. She's so rarely known boys. Girls have humiliated her in public places; it's a wonder she still tolerates the open air.

After dumping stones and coins in the largest of the two fabric bags, a tiny tear opens into a rent. A multitude of small things falls onto their feet.

Her father has been away for a while, too long, and she wonders now, finally, where he really is. An insane asylum? A dry-out place? Both her parents drink too much. The children have been left to their own devices.

What exactly are hers?

She thinks the things teenagers are supposed to think, but knows she's not fooling anyone. She doubts she'll ever feel the way a teenager is supposed to feel.

He is on his knees, his fingers on the things while she watches. From above he is just curly black hair. She lets him grovel at her feet. Many moments have passed since she last thought about being a twin.

He realizes that with these hoarded things, she means not just to hold onto herself but to achieve fame. She wears very dark, very large glasses whenever she leaves a building and walks out onto a street.

She's desperate to know the moments that hatched the sundering of their twin-ness. Was it remote? Violent? Cozy? What was her father doing? And for that matter, her mother? Did she push or did the girls just slip out, small as they were?

She knows they were never joined, except through their mother. But isn't that enough?

Now it's as if that other girl has disappeared, hardly a breath's mist, not even a pebble.

The father he carries around with him tries to get the boy to do something there in the closet. The father is speaking to him in a gruff, cajoling voice that holds itself in against violence.

She used to tell people they were originally Siamese. *Then they cut us apart, at the head, right here.* She would pull her hair away to show people a place on her scalp. It was nothing but people always said, *yeah*, seeing something. *And here*, she'd say, pulling down her sock and pointing to a place rubbed almost raw by the wrong shoes.

The father says: One, two, three.

The father says: Go!

The boy keeps his hands in his pockets looking down at his shoes covered in stones and coins.

Dad, you're not watching, are you?

He arches back then curls forward, over the girl and her many objects, spent and finally a man.

He prays without knowing how for something different, if not better, in the future. His feet are mired in the things she emptied there.

Their eyes are looking out the window that takes in the sky and nothing else. Without the window, her closet would be doomed. They stand on chairs, waiting for something to pass by. Kite, balloon, plane, man, bird.

Living here, they still startle at low-flying anything. That was when they were twelve. Now, they're almost adults. The city calls to them, a yearning they can't help but reciprocate.

"Let's go out for coffee," she says, and they leave the many pebbles, mostly grey or beige, but more variegated if you really look.

It's only a Starbucks and the girls from school, a rancid bunch, are clustered there. Ordering a frappucino, she wonders if they can tell just by looking at her mouth, but doesn't make a gesture to suggest a thing.

She notices the girls not noticing, their slim necks and wrists set at interesting angles. Bracelets sing, mouths jangle, absorbed and unrelenting. Cell phone tunes mix above the non-stop huff of milk being steamed. The girls' hair is strange, set apart from their bodies, almost separate nations. They won't look at her and she looks at them only in a swift glance that's required as she repositions herself. She and the boy walk out onto the ice and for a minute she loves him: "Do you think they still think I'm gross and fat?"

Now that he needs some advice, the father's voice is silent. The man is probably smoking one of his fat cigars.

"I think they don't think anything. They're premature. They only know to strut and cluck."

He looks at her, to his left, as they walk south on the east side of the street. He lets her take the inside part of the sidewalk because someone once told him to. The sun in his eyes makes him smile at it or at her, they're holding cold drinks on a cold day, the sun shining down onto sparkling ice.

"Careful," he tells her, grabbing her jacket and the arm underneath. "Don't slip," he says, suddenly sure of himself and the thing that went between them. The people on the street go around them, now that they're touching. He thinks of the scattered things they left behind on the closet floor. She's got on her green-edged sunglasses, almost famous—they're both amazed at how little it takes.

Courting Monsters

Watching Monsters

Monsters are generally large and somehow grotesque—the look of them disgusts us. This was so with her, I must admit. I almost couldn't look, and would have preferred to keep my eyes on an object in the far distance. Instead, I clapped them on her and watched some other part of myself try to turn away.

She let her eyes go to a far point in the room and I was free to examine the way her flesh hung, the way her once-beautiful face was misshapen, her skin large-pored and pasty, her once-wild hair now sparse and dyed a hue bearing no resemblance to anything in nature. Watching monsters is a sad business; I looked away.

Momentum

What did I hate during all those months? Why did the mention of that name put me on edge? I can say only this, that the act of making someone into a monster has its own momentum, start to finish.

Euphoria

Isn't it a contrived euphoria to believe in the other person's evil?

The creation of monsters can be a lifelong distraction.

Monster from Enemy?

How does a monster differ from an enemy? An enemy speaks of competition between equals. With monsters, there's no equality.

A monster is outlandish and has different-from-human qualities. Enemies exist; monsters don't. We invent monsters to let out parts of ourselves we find indigestible or at the very least unbecoming.

PITIFUL

In the liquid realm of dream, monsters come and go, turn seducer or hero. How many heroic, seductive qualities in any monster? And when the monster has been slain, how to control our tears, our pity?

SOME FAMOUS ONES:

Minotaur
Scylla and Charybdis
Sphinx
Sirens
Centaur

Monsters that disgust, seduce, kill, paralyze.

MEASUREMENTS

Are monsters merely what's familiar in an exaggerated form?

Monsters are often fat, though there are thin monsters as well. Some of them are see-through, or mostly see-through, just a thick elementary vein visible through clear flesh.

The heft of monsters is a weight that holds us rapt through the day. Sometimes, I admit, there's just no living without them.

COVER-UP?

What are the precise dimensions of this monster?

While obviously large, huge even, are there qualities of smallness? Does she, for instance, hide something very small internally? A small heart? A thinness to some layers of fiber? Cells smaller than most?

Everything visible is larger-than-life, conversation-stopping. It's only when she leaves the room that our mouths start moving again.

Relief?

Do we miss the monster or are we relieved that it's gone away?

There's an absorbent quality to monsters, like very thick paper towels.

Flattery

Am I a figment in the monster's imagination? (Or is the assumption mere self-flattery?)

Starving

Monsters, almost without exception, are voracious.

So is she a monster or a human being? Is she a cannibal or merely hungry? Is she huge because she eats to get at the meaning of life? Does it eternally evade her? Is it monstrous to allow such emptiness to show?

Like her, I've become monstrous in my appetite: this game never ends.

Legendary

If a monster is a person, then it can't be a monster. I guess I'm inventing her. With that enormous body, that insouciant method, she's become the stuff of legend.

Deciphering Monsters

We want monsters cleared from the fields—these urban fields we till and water and harvest.

What part of any monster is animal? What part howls and bites, cursing in a language we can't decipher?

This isn't the first time I've known a monster: in fact, I can't think of a time when I've been without.

A City Monster

Where do monsters sleep? In the old days, they lived on mountain tops, in caves, or at the bottom of the sea. This one occupies the city. Sometimes, even, she *is* the city. She's unnatural, awake with the dark, asleep with the sun.

Or is she just a poor fat thing with an excised husband and a scrawny, whiny daughter? A big girl with a sad story, a taste for grease and an inability to follow through?

Truth

This monster could be turned person in a second but something in me refuses to budge. This stubborn intolerance is monstrous. *I* am.

Pity

Pity dilutes a monster. When it's gone, I'm able to remember the person she once was.

And what about *her* monsters? (Probably far more interesting than mine.) What do monsters do when we're not thinking about them?

Muddy Floors

Even as we speak, monsters are tracking mud across clean floors. The truth, of course, is that no floor is as clean as we'd like to believe it is.

Ginka's Perfume

Ginka bustles her way through the kitchen, knocking pans together and using vast amounts of soapy water.

Her metal teeth—a whole corner of them—are not just shiny but exquisite. I wouldn't mind a couple of them myself.

This morning, as I walked upstairs from the garage, the sound of my steps was masked by the vacuum cleaner. My arrival at the top of the stairs frightened her. She grabbed me quickly, hugged me. Now, wherever I go, whatever I do, I've got her perfume here, a little stab from my right shoulder.

THEFT

Ginka stops working for a minute to tell me that, at the beginning of the summer, when tourists were starting to fill up the hotel where she sometimes works, Mr. Yannis (owner and proprietor) stole a bag left for her by the people in Room Four. The plastic bag was filled with bruised peaches, a yogurt or two, some rice. Filled, she emphasizes, with things they wanted me to have.

"So," she says, "I went to Mr. Yannis, I went right up to him like this" (she comes close but not too close, facing me) "and I said, 'Mr. Yannis, not that I want to stoop so low as to request my bag of broken and bruised things, but you're not the one who cleans the rooms, are you?'"

Then she turns on her heel and goes back to work.

Danger

Another day, she called to me, grabbed my hand, pointed to the snake in among the fallen pink-and-white petals of the bougainvillea.

I went at it with the broom and small as it was, it raised its head, twisted around and lunged for me.

My husband killed it with the broom handle as it tried to slink into a hole between the stones. But only after he'd finished his lunch.

In the Square

She said: "A man came up to my husband and asked where he was from."

"Bulgaria," he replied.

The man looked at him in a sly, proud way and asked: "Do you have television there? Electricity? Running water? Fresh fruit?"

My husband said, "Why no, we've got none of those things. Why, we haven't even got a sun."

The satisfaction on the man's face changed to dismay.

"You haven't got a sun?"

"No," her husband replied. "A pity, isn't it?"

Then she told me that her shiny teeth date from a fall she took in school. On that side of her mouth, all the teeth were knocked out.

Fish

We're absolutely firm: the smell of fish disgusts us. Neither of us eats it, ever.

Ginka and I are astonished to discover how much unites us; of course it's shocking all the things that divide us. Her silver teeth, for instance. And my inability to voice the certainty that they were once gold.

AT THE CROSSROADS

She said: "I saw you at the crossroads two days ago but I was too embarrassed to call out. My husband had been paid that day, so he took me to the café—a treat. As we sat there, Mr. Yannis came up and said: 'Look who's here! She doesn't have coffee in her house but she has money to go out for coffee!' Loudly! In front of everyone! I put my head down and felt tiny."

SILVER

Some mornings in the car, with the sun hitting them from the east, her teeth speak to me before she does.

PORTRAIT

That morning, she complained about the cough that wouldn't let go. The sea came over the cement edge of the harbor road and flooded their house. Once the salt got in, nothing ever dried completely.

Later that morning, drinking coffee, she told me that she has everything she wants, everything she needs. She said: "Everything you have here, I have at home. A washing machine, refrigerator, everything."

And then, as if to prove her point, that night, I found myself in her house for the first time. A poor house. Clean, of course, with little knick-knacks around.

When we arrived, she was already black-clad, sitting outside on a chair, holding onto a framed photograph of her older son.

LULLABY

On the way to the graveyard, she wailed and screamed and sang him a little song that went up and down, almost a lullaby.

Through the crowd, I saw her hands on her dead son's bruised, yellow face.

WIND

The next week, she said: "Didn't I tell you that when the wind came and blew the windows and door, something had happened? Something was strange in the world." She said: "Didn't I tell you?"

SILVER FOR GOLD

A day or so after the funeral, the dead son's girlfriend told Ginka that she was pregnant. It turns out that she wasn't. But this girlfriend, Ginka says, once accused the son of beating her. The woman had faced Ginka and said: "If you don't pay me, you'll visit your son in jail."

So, it turns out, she traded her gold teeth for a set of silver ones.

BLESSING

After he died, she said: "That everyone may be well."

Meaning, everyone in the world.

RUINS

Another couple of weeks passed before I remembered something she'd said to me on that day, the day of his death: "Neighbors from my village in Bulgaria came and told me that my mother's house is a ruin."

She stopped wiping the windows, looked at me, and said: "And one day, our houses too will be ruins. It's the way things go."

Twenty-nine Stones for You to Hold

The Shepherd

The group of students came upon the shepherd in his grassy valley near the small umber-colored chapel. They'd been hiking since dawn; it was now nearly eleven. The sun was high, accompanied by a breeze that shifted the tall grasses around the shepherd. They watched him lean against his crook as if it were a movie.

He kept his eye on his sheep and the land—craggy with sharp rocks, orange earth, and a steep incline just beyond the grassy knoll. The students were heading toward the sea; they had a long way to go, all descent. They pulled oranges from their knapsacks and one of the girls offered hers to the shepherd. Shyness kept him from taking it.

Within moments, most of the girls wanted to marry him. The boys wanted to *be* him, to grab the life out from under him and keep it. One of the girls imagined making a tiny slit in the atmosphere, and pulling him away from his life in the mountains where he herded sheep day and night, leaning against thick olive trunks while the sheep grazed.

Americans are rarely shy. They came out with the words: "We want to BE you!" The shepherd stared at the earth.

Some of them wondered whether he was all there, so apparently immune was he to the students' frantic desires.

Leaving, they kept their gaze forward. All of them wanted to look back; none of them did. As if they'd come upon him naked, they were eager to restore his modesty.

Sony Hand-held

From the spot where Yakovos had stuck the knife into the ram's neck, a torrent flowed down over the dry orange earth and the molten-looking rocks. It made a rivulet that approached our feet.

One boy asked: "Is our blood thick like that?" I answered that any blood, against such dry earth and with a 90-degree sun beating down on it, would probably coagulate quickly. From the original gash, blood had spurted not once but twice in a forward jet that forced us all to move.

That boy took pictures with a three-by-five inch silver rectangle. He showed me where the lens was, then aimed at the bloody ram's head just above us and took a picture. While I looked at it on the screen, he said: "I can delete it, if I want."

We watched as Yakovos made a small cut in the skin of the thigh, then blew air into the space between skin and flesh, eventually adding another balloon-like third to the original animal. Next, he sliced wool and skin away from flesh. Once the animal's chest cavity was open, exposing the range of guts, the boy got busy showing me other things his machine could do. It had a calendar, games, and a lot of the latest songs. He filled in his datebook while the men removed liver, spleen, stomach and heart.

Marker

The mark in the road was an uneven pile of stacked rocks. Passing, I laughed. I figured that someone was sending a little message. It made me chuckle. A small pile of granite rocks, orange-and-grey in color, rising. I liked what I saw. You would have, too.

It was two days before my eyes finally went where the marker directed them: across the road, high in the rocks, a black lamb hung down, its neck caught in a narrow chasm.

I'm not saying that God made the marker. And obviously, it wasn't an art project. But there was no denying its beauty.

BARREL DOG

I love the way that dog, chained to the barrel, guarding those new chicks, lies on his side, back legs straight bones, his testicles a tight round bulb (almost garlic-like) facing the sun, and me, as I pass, not so furtively, on my way home.

A CASE IN POINT

Old Spiros saw me coming up the hill and asked if I'd seen any sheep on the road. The animals should have been up the mountain by then, late afternoon.

I said: "I don't think so, but then, since I see your sheep on the road every single day, my brain" (tapping it once) "sets them there right now. So I can't tell you for sure."

Even with shepherds, one sometimes needs to refer to the brain and its exigencies. I'm still not sure he followed, but his face contorted into something like a smile.

BURNING BOOKS

All afternoon, the wind has blown from the north, snowflakes passing horizontally across the windows, our world turned sideways. We'd had no expectation of such cold: the firewood is nearly gone. If it doesn't let up, we'll have to start burning our library.

You know how dearly we love these books, but we're practically freezing!

SHIT IN THE ROAD

There are days when the pattern of animal shit in the road is the most interesting thing around, and these are not bad days.

EGGS

Kostis has been giving us so many eggs we can't figure out what to do with them. I know he throws half a dozen to the barrel dog at the edge of his field. Every few days there's a mess of yolk and shell thrown on top of a half-gnawed loaf of bread. Some days that skinny dog has so much to eat, he leaves the mess for later.

GATHERING SALT

Early mornings in late July, the shepherds and their wives gather by the edge of the sea to collect salt. They wear canvas shoes and jump between sharp rocks—people sprain their ankles collecting salt, though you wouldn't think of it as a dangerous activity.

If you know a little about the sun and the vast, increasingly filthy sea, you can gather enough salt to last the year. Or sell it to gourmet markets for a decent price.

But salt isn't the only thing gathered and taken home for free: When a ship far out at sea is wrecked and loses its cargo, that cargo, whether it's cases of Japanese-made dolls or porcelain bowls, becomes the property of the finder.

I remember the autumn when hundred-pound sacks of shredded coconut washed up on the rocks. No one knew what it was. By winter, the women were using it in every dish—cakes and cookies, soups, sauces. They added it to everything but their hallowed meat, always pure with just a pinch of salt.

THIEF

That woman in the lower village keeps denying that she's got our peahen. And yet we can see her, right there beyond the olive trees, scrabbling around with the woman's chickens, locked in the cage.

NATIONAL HIGHWAY

The boy on the motorcycle tried to make the National Highway continue beyond its present boundary. Speeding, he went over the metal guard with its puny reflectors and fell to his death in the pit containing what will one day be the continuation of the National Highway.

Since then, the metal guard has been upgraded: now there are foot-long diagonal reflector lines. For a week after his death, a new red light pulsed. The flowers have dried up but the red ribbons dance in the wind, the silver florist paper's still shiny.

CRACKED RIB

I never really knew whether the rib was cracked, but I did have pneumonia and it made me cough a ghastly cough.

The old bone woman insisted that it was cracked. The legend was that she'd borne eight children and repaired every one of their broken bones with her own concoctions. The concoctions weren't hers exclusively but what she'd learned as a girl from the original bone woman on the island.

She slathered olive oil across my ribs as if I were lamb flesh and soaked an Ace bandage in ouzo. She wrapped it around my torso and told me to leave it there until I was cooked.

Eventually it stopped hurting; I never went for a follow-up.

CYCLOPS

Spiros, the cyclops, as my husband calls him, is not exactly a village idiot. His intelligence reaches the requirement for a shepherd, though it doesn't exceed it by even one degree. He's friendly to me; one wouldn't call it friendship. Sometimes I hear him from beyond the bend in the road where atop his tractor he screams hysterically at his animals as if they were bad wives or clever siblings. When I reach him, his blind eye holds steady and the real one looks at me. I want to say: Keep your good eye on the road!

WHITE RABBIT

My husband knew the smell. It wasn't until four in the afternoon, sun still high, that he found the source: a white rabbit, fatly pregnant, all the little teats still swollen. He lobbed it across the wire fence into Skarakis' land.

It was June. The wind and driving rain wouldn't come for another three months. We'd have to live with the smell.

THE PATIENT GOAT

Have you ever seen a goat take a running start in order to get up a steep incline? It was a full-sized goat, a she. When I came around the bend, I saw the two other goats, one large and one a kid go up fast, without a hitch. They stood on a ledge of rock, not exactly waiting. She tried to follow them but couldn't go beyond a certain point. It wasn't a great distance, only ten feet or so, but the incline stopped her. She went downhill backwards.

The second time, she took a running start. I watched her strain at the same point as she had before but this time she made it.

PERFECT CREATURE

The lamb's hoofs were fully formed. In fact, the entire lamb was there, nothing out of place, just that it was obviously undernourished. At first we thought it'd been born earlier that morning, maybe around four, and in the rain. It looked like a runt, though as far as we know, it was the ewe's only newborn. There could have been others left on the mountain.

Later, holding the lamb against my chest, I saw what was left of the umbilical cord—shrivelled and dried—and knew the lamb had probably followed its mother around on the part of the mountain we can't easily see from here, until starving (she was a first-time mother), its knees buckled and it stayed in that spot until he found it.

But it was all there, a perfect creature, the hoofs hard and forthright, ready to stomp as its mother did every time we came near. Two hours later it was dead. He buried it under an olive tree.

Rabbit

The day we discovered rabbits everywhere, I felt sorry for them and wanted them all to escape. He made me hold a big stick right beside the hole while he chased them back into the cage. Still, there was a big white mother we couldn't capture. Some mornings I find her staring at me, just beyond the window while I type.

Flaming Rats

The rat extinguisher told us that the best way to rid the place of rats is by catching one, dousing it with gasoline, then setting it on fire and letting it run as far as it can go. By the time it's burned to death, the other rats in the area will have heard its screeches of terror. They'll stay away, he said, for at least five generations.

Firewood

He opened the church door that morning because the sun was finally out. From that height, he could see the women, one in beige and burgundy, the other in cream and brown, walk back to the village carrying neat piles of twigs on their shoulders. As they moved down the road past fields of olive trees, the wood stacked on their shoulders merged with the trees for quick seconds, then became distinct.

Peahen Returned

Themistocles arrived with the peahen in the seat beside him in the dirty white Volkswagen bug. He'd forgotten to tie her claws and when he opened the door, she hopped out. She'd been gone for over four months, on a visit to the lower village and that foreign woman's roosters. My husband was overjoyed to have his peahen back, even though it's the cocks that are beautiful. Scrawny and brownish, there's nothing beautiful to her.

All the next day, the peacock chased her, suddenly pulling up short, making exorbitant displays of his beauty. He must have won her over—the next day their motions were more ordinary, his calls blasé.

Shoot

That new Sifi, just retired and back to the village until he dies, hangs a rifle from his shoulder every morning, tracking wild hare in the grapevines below the house. Every morning, orange sunrise tinting his face and mine, I call out, startling him. He steps away from the broken wire fence and insists: "I'm not out to shoot partridges, just the odd hare or two."

I'm afraid that one of these mornings he'll shoot *me*.

The Yorgos

Once again, one Yorgo wanted to kill the other Yorgo, because of the sheep.

The one Yorgo's sheep were mostly white and clean. A recent short hard rain had rinsed the matted fur of the past summer's orange earth. The fences had gone down in the storm and before the other Yorgo could fix them, the sheep crossed into his land. Without fences, sheep follow the green.

That Yorgo went after each sheep craftily, lunging at the right moment and bringing the knife across the neck. He left the animals to bleed and die. No one would eat them: wasted effort. The other Yorgo's, not his.

BUCOLIC

When the sun shines on their grassy patch and those yellow buttercups are plentiful, it's easy to be awed by the ewes, their lambs snuggled into the crook of their limbs. But I'm not fooled: anything with a pea-brain can sit aimless and bewitched in the sun for hours.

ABSCESS

Yorgia's mouth was rancid with abscess. Not one of her grandchildren would let her come near. Collecting eggs from the field, the tooth throbbed when she inclined her head. Even the hens scrambled away across the lumpy earth.

PETER

When my husband arrives at the cage, they all come running. Some of the young ones, all white, stay near him. But once they've felt his touch, they run away—all but Peter, who is black and recognizable. He turns smaller and rounder in my husband's kind hand.

SPRING

Yesterday the man brought the new piglet. He parked his truck in the driveway and, seeing me through the doorway of our house, called out: "Do you have a piece of cloth I could use? The pig shat and I can't grab hold because it's slippery."

I went outside and pointed to an empty animal food sack. "Will that do?" "Yes," he said, and wiped his hand on it then clamped his hand over the piglet's curly tail, grabbed a pink, sensitive-looking ear and hoisted it over the side of the truck. He carried it that way for two hundred yards. I kept thinking the pig would slip from his grip but it didn't.

The piglet went directly to the much larger sow. She didn't flinch or run away but stood still, knee-deep in slops. The sun was warmer than it'd been in months. The little pig nuzzled her tail and each of her trotters, and eventually her snout. They ate side by side, slurping. Later, we found them lying together as the sun went down, the piglet snuggled into her belly, her head against his.

GOLDEN HANDS

When I went to pick up the plate of *boureki* Fofo had promised my husband, she showed me the family photographs then pointed out the various cracks in the ceiling. She indicated a chair in the kitchen and whirled around, reaching for high shelves. She put a small glass plate before me, spooned a curl of yellow bergamot preserve onto it. Added syrup and gave me a tiny spoon. A tall glass of perfectly cold water. Poured a shot of what she called cherry liqueur.

Sitting down with me, she announced: "All these things are from my own hands." I asked: "Where do I begin?" She laughed and said: "Wherever you like." So I took a sip of the red liqueur, found it tasty and told her so, then used the edge of my tiny spoon to cut into the tough bergamot, put it in my mouth and savored the springy texture of the fruit against the syrup's sweetness. The fruit has a flavor like perfume. I couldn't describe my mouth's confusion beneath the fluorescent rods of her kitchen lighting, but I hope she heard the slight rapture in my voice as I congratulated her on the success of her "golden hands."

GOATS

The difference between my village and New York? Here, when you go out to look at some faces, it's always the same ones, and most of them furred.

At the end of my stay in that hotel, I took all the notepads. Who could imagine the lists that would be recorded on those pages? The things I'd need to do. To remind myself to think about. To buy.

People to call. Returning to the village with so many stolen pads seemed to assure me of a busy autumn.

And thinking back: How many such pages have already lined the digestive tracts of various hungry goats? The herd that live near the garbage dump nibble on broken machinery as well as the odd piece of paper. Perhaps that's why goat, boiled or roasted, is so much tastier than lamb, which thrives on grass and grain, nothing spicier.

SIGNS

The moment I thought to jot down some notes for you, a partridge flew out from the early spring grass and crossed my path. The bird made its pretty cooing squawk and headed east toward the sun. I figured the moment auspicious.

CAFFEINE

This is a conversation with my insides. The instigator? Pain. Some days it's worse than others; most days it's just above neutral, persistent, yet almost not there at all.

The purpose of this tedious pain must be either to cleanse me or prepare me. But for what?

Sometimes the pain is invisible; sometimes it outlines parts of my body in white light. Some days it feels like trapped air. Other days, I imagine lacerations, like a rug burn. Occasionally I feel like sticking a long pin into the place where throat and stomach meet. Something is awry, needs help.

A small white pill opens a door and very gently escorts the pain outside. The lit-up parts of me go dark, unseen, forgotten.

For months before discovering the pill, I couldn't fall asleep without my husband's help.

I pop a few roasted soy beans into my mouth. Their skins are like parchment or flower petals left too long between the pages of a book. I crush the beans with my teeth, hold the skins on my tongue.

I'm trying to understand the way something I hold in my hand or mouth becomes part of the hand, the mouth.

Dreamt that a thick layer of my tongue was coming off. A tongue, used for speaking as well as chewing.

What was it with those Sweet 100s? I ate one tomato and another and another until the basket was empty. Like tear-drops, or fresh-water pearls, something precious to take inside.

Appetite fires you to eat all you can without a modicum of measure. Then, you're punished by digestion's slow torture.

Greedy enough to swallow the whole earth, you experience a moment of deep fear: How am I edible? What greater thing could eat me?

Human, animal, weather-pattern, god. All of the above?

With sickness concocting me, my best stories are all broken. I used to be able to say: When I was young. And: In the days before our children were born, my husband and I.

Now, only one story remains, the tale of sickness, greedy to upstage any other: this pain where stomach meets throat.

This is how you reach nirvana: Quit drinking coffee for two months, then fall off the wagon. Three sips and your mind sees shapes it's forgotten existed. It hums with song, color, and the immense realization: you hold the thread that sews the world together.

I remember the city of my birth at the winter solstice. We walked beside the ocean, the full moon rising. We crawled inside a dune and ate each other up. (With such a meal, eating and digestion are seamless.) Afterwards, we held our hands above a bonfire, backs damp with wind-borne salt water.

You take three small sips of coffee and scan for results. (Any additional gut noise, a touch of thickened saliva?) This is an inversion of appetite, watching X-ray-like as the things descend.

Do you really think your brain can control the way food is digested, the way the body incorporates parts of the world? Will obsessive watching let you swallow the universe? Isn't this your aim? To take everything inside?

The incessant gurgle of acid eating away at my insides, followed by pain, forces me to realize that I must stop drinking coffee.

Coffee fine-tunes my psyche, jump-starts my brain. Without it, I can't manufacture an audience.

No listener? No point in talking.

Without speech, I'm stuck with all the quickly-swallowed, undigested chunks.

I'll miss my high-flying brain.

This is the draw of a café: stoked on caffeine, you make the world as you watch it.

Green tea: a drink that tastes of the dark sea. Nothing close to coffee's bitter earthiness.

⁂

Dreamt I was stuck in an elevator with a mass of words stuck to my tongue. Unable to spit them out or swallow them, I prayed the door would open on a familiar face.

⁂

I picture the pained parts of me huddled together, full of desire, hungry and uncomfortable. They call to me like small children, impossible to ignore. Throttling them won't work.

I can't take pills the rest of my life; neither can he fuck me to sleep every night.

⁂

Infinity: the narcotic promise I can't resist.

⁂

I encourage my mind to fall apart in my hand. How to put the pieces back together?

⁂

I drink yerba mate, a tea from another country. It tastes of saddles and animal sweat. One sip takes me to another century. For several days, I find relief, then the pain begins again, more insistent than before. Historical-remove provides no answer. I can't escape my century, my country, my life. (My stomach.)

⁂

I digest my days with words.

⁂

Unwritten days feel dammed. Occasionally, the dam breaks: all the uncooked things come loose. I drown in the undigested dregs of my life.

With a caffeine-stoked brain, I can turn the handle at my own pace, let water through the floodgate to equalize the pressure. Between written and unwritten, told and untold, real and imagined. How else to hold a life in your hand? How else to say your prayers?

He leaves for a night; I wake up twenty times and then stop counting.

We all have to put up with our minor aches and pains. But why the desperation to make them into minor works of art?

Fumbling generosity? Awkward substitution? Of milk, for instance, and a mother's arms?

When my mother falls on the carpeted stairs of her house, she tells me on the phone that the injury is only slight.

I buy small things for her, aiming for a less that means more: five miniature chocolate bars, a tiny glass globe, a plastic watch.

At her house, I see that her hand is very swollen, with a bluish gash. She says: "It's only my circulation." She smiles: "Or lack thereof."

I give her the things, knowing they don't come close to saying what I mean.

Hands trace feeling along muscles and nerves, release pain, send it downstream, as if it were a feisty fish. My massage therapist tells me she gives the massage she'd like to receive. In this way, I come to know her particular aches and pains, and desires.

I know she likes to have her shoulder blades pulled away from the back, as if they're wings. She likes the fascia between to be pressed and pulled. I like this too, her desires meeting my own. Like a small rebirth, a non-sexual fling.

She works as if she's cooking: pinch and fold, stir and mix. She exerts pressure that reaches a variety of levels: nerve, muscle, bone, cell.

After the massage, I eat a donut, iced. Each bite a taunt, a test of my stomach's health.

Need all pain be significant? Only to those who believe in the efficacy of an intellectual unraveling. Is this cerebral voodoo? High-minded witchcraft? Or simply the luxury of one fortunate enough to have a minor pain, rather than a drastic, insupportable one?

I requested deep, hard. For the duration of fifty minutes, he made me hurt.

These places I go: a tiny closet office, big enough for a wooden table and a smiling Buddha, where he pummels me. His hands call forth colors I usually never wear, but there's relief in being dressed this way, naked beneath his hands. He keeps me too long and I rush away, dropping three stiff twenties on the table.

Can thought be nourishing? Can one grow fat on thoughts?

Ethereal pains are the most difficult to describe. A twinge, then nothing. A quick stab and it's gone. Like our awareness of mortality. Even when steeped in it, the comprehension never exceeds *slight*.

I cradle the pain in my mind, and it dissolves. When I see how this works, I think of my mother and know how badly I want to give her something good.

I dream things I haven't thought of in years: intense summer blues, infinitely tall pine trees, the yellow of corn on the cob. Images leak back to their holding place beneath my diaphragm.

My mother and I happen to be in the same market at the same time, but I have to shout before she recognizes me. She's looking for peaches; I'm buying lettuce and carrots.

I notice that the gash on her hand looks better—relief.

For a week, I conjure the pain—like a punch to the esophagus—with thoughts of a double espresso. Eventually my stomach realizes how it's been fooled: there's nothing to fear from a thought.

I sip strong coffee, trying to condition myself. When the bitterness hits, I'm already at that place, soothing the part with mumbled syllables—things you'd tell a dying parent, a crying child. Words like healing hands.

Early morning thunderstorm. The clarity of the light makes you want to eat the sky.

Perform tiny surgeries on your body, watching and feeling at once. Cut, bleed, suture, staunch. Notice the intricacy of your stitch-work, the miracle of its ensemble.

Inhale the light. Practice waving to your mother even when she can't see you.

Know how caffeine's an alibi.

BEING CONQUERED

A FOOT IN BOTH WORLDS

Before leaving home, I had one of those headaches that won't go away, no matter what you take. For three days, it plagued me. Then, when the plane touched down in Istanbul, it disappeared.

The purpose of the trip was pleasure. To me, it seemed like pure hubris. I feared the new place would pull us apart right where, after years of labor, we seemed finally, definitively joined. I was terrified.

My husband and I took a taxi from the airport to the edge of Europe where we looked across to Asia for the very first time.

I admit: having my feet in Europe and my eyes on Asia irresistible.

ODYSSEUS AND PENELOPE

The first afternoon, the two of us, like some Odysseus and his Penelope returned to one another after years apart, sat in the garden between two mosques: the ancient-looking former church of Ayia Sofia, her sad imperial red surface worn away, and the dashing, much younger Blue Mosque.

We watched worshippers as they left the mosque. Across from us, a man in a white skullcap read the Koran while his covered, blue-scarfed wife sat beside him—a little like us. The wife read along with her husband, but at a different pace. She'd read for a while then look up. From beneath her *feretze*, she seemed to look my way.

For the next several days, I'd watch women covered in what looked to be heavy clothing as they moved past in the street. Their long dark blue or grey dresses seemed cumbersome. But there's wisdom in such drapery: a woman can regard the world frankly, without being seen.

THEIR TROJAN WAR

Of what did those difficult years consist? The labors of a life: making children, feeding and clothing them, sending them off into the world.

Odysseus had his war, his Circes. Penelope raised young Telemachuses, wove and unwove her carpets. The suitors provided her with a war of her own.

Had she really snubbed every single one of them? (Did he never think of Nausikaa?)

COSTUME

I was reluctant to give up the costume of my own clothing, scorned taking off my shoes and wearing a borrowed scarf. Ilias was desperate to get inside the mosque, so I acquiesced. After removing our shoes, we crossed a wooden walkway, together with a horde of high school students from various places in Europe, all of them commenting in their own languages on the smell. Entering the mosque, I felt no older than these young people, and petulant. My hooded jacket would have to be a good-enough head-covering.

My Odysseus, man of adventure, walked into the Blue Mosque and seemed to swoon. Within a minute, he looked as if he was on the verge of converting.

It was easy to be enamored of the grandeur of the architecture, the decoration on the walls. I watched him fall into the endlessly repeated motifs, like a kind of love.

My jacket's hood fell away from my head; I left it that way. Someone's feet had to stay planted on the earth.

Eventually, we walked home through the Egyptian Market where, at the end of a long row of stalls, a seller stopped us, cut off pieces of *soutzouk* made of grape must and almonds, handed one to each of us. I loved the rubbery texture—it made me think I could chew forever. Ilias wouldn't touch it, never eats between meals.

One could imagine that my tastes ran toward gastronomic delights while his were loftier, spiritual, but in the crucible of a long marriage, identities get confused—there's really nothing so precise as a Penelope waiting at her loom and an Odysseus adventuring homeward over the course of ten long years.

BELIEVER

In mosques, you won't find a single face in the decoration unless you hallucinate one. There's a vast distinction between the humans praying on their knees and the high round dome covered in colorful design. It's design like a wordless song, an intricate hum.

But in the Greek Orthodox church of St. Sotir in Chora, Istanbul, the thirteenth-century frescoes contain human figures. Staring up at the walls, you're searched by eyes that don't look directly into yours but catch their gaze, then challenge you to follow toward a world beyond.

DESIRE

By the third day, we'd put our feet on each continent within a single twenty-four hour stretch. Europe and Asia. The proximity of the two land masses stirred desire—not just for each other, but for worlds beyond our reach. We ached for lives that could move arrow-like through time, spearing all the years we'd missed by an accident of birth.

It wasn't only the food we ate—puddings, lamb in various sauces, *kaimak* ice cream, jars of pickled cauliflower, onions, pineapple, pear, apple, pomegranate, quince—but the pool in the central hall of the sultan's summer palace, built not as a place for the sultan to swim but simply to provide the sound of water, an aural reminder of the quality of coolness.

Leaving near the servants' entranceway, Penelope caught up with Odysseus and touched his shoulder. Even Odysseus, wiliest adventurer, felt sad that he couldn't be a sultan. He sulked.

When they were back in a car heading across the bridge toward Europe, she watched Asia recede—he stayed under some Circe's spell.

BACKGAMMON

Odysseus went off to play backgammon with the Iranian rug seller; Penelope sat by a window to ruminate on the day's trajectory. It's easy, she thought, to want to dive back in time, especially when you're in Istanbul.

As the men slammed down their plastic pieces on black and red triangles, Penelope missed her home, their children; her parents, her grandparents, their grandparents. The villages where they'd lived five generations back. Places she didn't know the names of. People she'd never seen, even in photographs. She missed everything, all the way back to the beginning.

After Odysseus won three games out of five, she propelled him to their Istanbul home: a bed in a room draped in checkered carpets, itself a little like a backgammon board, but also not entirely different from a loom.

NEGLECT

Sometimes we were simply Ilias and Hannah. He explained to me how the Byzantine Empire was finally taken: when the Italian commander Justiniani was hit through the chest, his men lost heart and wouldn't carry on fighting. To prevent the possibility of desertion, the men were locked inside the city walls. In the chaos, a small back door was left open. The Sultan's men found it and entered. May 29, 1453, a Tuesday.

Just think: a whole empire routed through the neglect of a small back door.

One can't spend a lifetime attending every door, guarding all gates. Think of a marriage, like a small empire, with a window left innocently raised. Who knows what influences can come in on an afternoon breeze?

Since the Fall of the Empire, Greeks view Tuesdays with suspicion and fear. Ilias and I met on a Tuesday. While most view such a conjunction warily, we've found intriguing ways to tame ill winds. The concurrence is a talisman.

CROSSROADS

The small clear glasses of orange-colored tea are ubiquitous. Visible everywhere, they remind you of where you are: here, at a crossroads where east meets west, past meets present. The two of you in all your manifestations—Penelope, Hannah, Odysseus, Ilias, and others, unnamed—meet again, as if for the first time, after all these years.

RUGS

One afternoon we went out for coffee and returned with several rugs. The rugs, for sale every few steps as one walks through the city, are faceless creations like the decorated walls of the mosques.

The rugs' beauty is in the pattern and placement of color, a lively resting point for the mind amidst the statues and stones, the columns that stand watch over the ebb and flow of generations.

We bought several of them in un-dyed wool. It made me happy to know they'd accompany us to our home, souvenirs to welcome our future comings-and-goings.

ARRIVAL

Looking back as we walked across the Galata Bridge, we saw something extraordinary: the minarets beside the domes looked exactly like the images we'd seen in photographs. The pictures rose in our minds to tell us that what we beheld was actual, real.

It can take years to reach the place where desire spirals to fullness: the many departures finally become an overwhelming sense of having arrived.

Our lives rode our hearts, not a beat mislaid; we couldn't keep our hands to ourselves.

His Fingers

On the other side of the Golden Horn, Ilias told me that he couldn't remember a time when he hadn't thought about sultans, emperors, churches and mosques.

He could put his finger on exact dates: this dome, that wall. Across that bridge. Between those trees. He kept pointing: Do you see the crevice between those walls?

Ilias was open-handed with this plethora of new information; I fell into a stupor trying to grasp the depth of his knowledge.

History's nooks formed places in his mind. I wished I could step inside, walk around leisurely, get to know all the sultans and empresses, harem women, monks and craftsmen—all his acquaintances. To console myself, I thought about my loom, planned to people it with lively presences.

Music

At five-to-five, on our fifth day, the recorded *muezzin* came on. It touched something near the diaphragm, a spiritual locus in the body. In the old days, real chanters ascended the minaret five times daily.

The voices, though pre-recorded, played almost synchronously from a variety of mosques, weaving and folding, forming soft peaks and firm ones: a music to match the clouds over the Bosphorus or the domes of the Suleymaniye Mosque.

The beauty of the music made me desperate to create its equivalent in silk thread, though I feared it was close to impossible—like passing successfully between Scylla and Charybdis, waiting faithfully for one's husband to return from the wars, or raising heroic sons.

How They Whirled

In the octagonal room, we stood amongst foreigners who positioned and then repositioned their chairs, focusing their video cameras. Ilias leaned against a column while I stood near a window with a view of a garden. The musicians entered, made prayerful bows, took their seats, played, then exited and climbed stairs to where they took their place as religious players wearing mushroom-colored turbans.

The dervishes came in slowly, bowing, beginning to turn. Eventually, as the music crescendoed, they whirled. They wore white skirts, angled their heads to the right, one hand open, the other closed, as if touching both heaven and earth. The whirling, grounded in a quick movement of the feet you could see beneath the white skirts, opened out into spinning. It looked dreamy and difficult, then simply dreamy. Some of the boys made it look effortless, as if a god inhabited them. Others sweated and went out of their orbit; the chief dervish in black went close to reorient them.

After dinner and the ride back across the Bosphorus, we set foot once again on the European continent. It was becoming easy—a foot in both worlds. At our room in the hotel, with the lights turned low, he put his arms out and began to whirl. He went around twice, stopped, and nearly fell.

Then I, Hannah, put out my arms, one hand open to the heavens, the other toward the earth, and spun ten, twenty times, more than I could have imagined, so I became his planet, and my gravity drew him on. We fell into bed together, but delicately, like those hands, one in each direction.

That night I became many-named: Hannah and Penelope, along with unpronounceable, untranslatable names. Names composed of breath and mouth, throat.

We slept long past dawn, deaf to the *muezzin*. We awakened and dozed, drowsy with visions of the pillow-like domes that took the eye upward without the least bit of effort.

The sun was gathered against the red carpet when we finally stretched ourselves to meet the day.

AYIA SOFIA

The last day, we'd still not visited Ayia Sofia. We'd passed it often, walking through the square that seemed to divide the whole world: Ayia Sofia to the east, the Blue Mosque to the west.

That day dawned white and cold. Inside the church, Ilias was lost in contemplation of the fall of an empire. It was as if a beloved member of his family had died, someone I'd heard about but never met. I walked alone.

My sadness was different, not large enough to embrace an entire history, empires, continents. We walked together and apart in the huge, drafty church, sharing the scuffed floor with others, each intent on his own exploration of the battered church. Beneath the dome that had witnessed massacres and desecration as well as boundless faith, I wanted merely to hold his hand, be held by his, and then to leave that place together.

But he left first. I stayed on a few minutes, walking in the vast space created by that dome. The building was extraordinary, a whole universe within its walls. I tried to see what he had seen, but knew no amount of effort would show me; I could know only my own mind.

Twirling Dervishes

Travelling: Abstract

What happens when you arrive in a country and, walking along streets full of shops, there's nothing you want to buy?

You have no desire to hand over your dollars or euros or pounds in exchange for a scarf, a watch, a bottle of perfume, or an antique lamp.

It's not that you want to hold onto your money—there's simply nothing you want in its place.

This isn't austerity but a muting of want; it's the disinterment of capitalism, right in your own psyche.

Country: Turkey

From the other room, I hear my son ask: "Is it *whirling* dervishes or *twirling*?"

Whirling; Psychology

Bring your cameras (but don't use your flash). Sneeze, if necessary, but observe quiet. Don't squirm or fuss. This is a religious ceremony put on for your benefit. Observe (or, alternately, close your eyes). Let your eyes rest on the graceful whirling of dervish, a heretical cult, a religious offshoot, a show. Watch their young faces opening to another world. Watch them touch their heads to the wooden floor. Wonder what goes on inside the head of a fifteen-year-old who whirls.

CAPITALISM; HUNGER

Two mosques yesterday? No, three. This, too, is consumption. It's a kind of buying even if no money changes hands.

Buying another's religion: visiting mosques, watching dervishes whirl.

Everything's about hunger—the halt and hold of it, the control and appeasement of it.

SULTANS; BODIES OF WATER; CAMERAS

Our comments through the Dolmabahce Palace were mostly sarcastic, facetious. How to take seriously such opulence?! A magnificence of size and proportion! The Sultan's official area and private quarters were luxurious and well-kept; the harem, where the women and children lived, was shoddy. The dirty pink walls hadn't been painted in years, there were cracks in the ceiling.

But the view to the Bosphorus took our breath away. The light, the dazzle of sun on briskly-moving water that went to the Black Sea in one direction and out to the Marmara in the other. A passage to all worlds, just beyond the Palace's side gate.

The view to the Bosphorus was the only thing in that palace I wanted to eat.

But others were hungry, snapping away, all the familiar pings in our common machines, our technological devices.

EMPIRES; CONQUERED PEOPLES; BEGGARS

The beggars seemed to find our tall son a likely candidate for spare change. He simply walked on, silent, or sometimes turned to me and

171

said something in Greek, rather loudly, trying to give the beggar a message, I suppose, about empires and their demise.

MAP: STREET, SQUARE, TULIPS

The day of our arrival, Taxim Square was thick with SWAT teams. There'd been a bomb on a bus.

The next day, Istiklal was crazy with passersby. Taxim Square was newly-planted with tulips.

ISLAM; EYELESS FACES

Walking through the Eyup Mosque, I was barefoot but not bareheaded in a crush of women, fingers pointed heavenward, palms facing inward, eyes back in their heads. No one twitched an eye, much less followed me with a glance. They gazed somewhere inside, toward a place I don't know, or maybe don't have.

Even if tinged with resentment, a glance would've been preferable to the otherworldly eyeless faces that had no place for anything not godly.

COUNTRY: GREEN

Green is a color I've always associated with the outdoors—plants, trees, all shades and tones in a harmonious orchestration. Since that glimpse of Eyup's all-green tomb, the color has become a country I once visited without passport or method, barefoot, with only a headscarf to guide me.

Where is the green in my heart?

NAVIGATION: GEOGRAPHICAL, PSYCHOLOGICAL

The tricky navigation of this turbulent water between narrow straits. All of us and our private Symplegades.

TRAVEL; MIRRORS

At the hotel, there were mirrors on every wall. My body met me everywhere I looked. Eventually, I became disenchanted with a body that generally pleases me. My best self dissolved in the ubiquity of truth-telling mirrors; my pride went too. Then, I wrote a letter to M.

EMPIRES; LOSS; MUSTAPHA AND ALI

M.—I want you to know that we did our best to procure old candle wax from St. Mary of the Mongols. Along the way, we got lost amongst the fundamentalists with their women's covered heads, many plastic red-and-white flags, bathroom-tile-on-the-outside houses. Set on treacherous winding cobbled streets, we wound our way up and down and up again without coming upon anything resembling a Byzantine church.

The map always showed that it was just around the next bend. We swore and perhaps even prayed in our fervor to find the oldest Byzantine church in Istanbul that's remained in Greek hands, but to no avail. Eventually, young Mustapha with sidekick Ali appeared in their school uniforms, asked where we were going. I said: "Church!" And they led us there.

But it was a Wednesday, lunchtime, and after banging on iron doors and pressing bells, a man stuck his head out of a nearby window and said: "*Dimanche!*" so we understood that we'd failed, and left without taking a picture or gathering a little of the grass that grew like weeds between the paving stones that led up to the steps of St. Mary of the Mongols, poor now and mostly abandoned.

So, M.—We failed to bring back a notion of the church but looking for it gave us what, I think, anyone comes here to find: a feeling of melancholy that grows huge in the monumental space of all that's been lost.

FUNDAMENTALISTS; HEADSCARF

Fundamentalist politicos handed me a small, cheaply-made book, and this was before I'd draped a scarf over my hair.

PATRIARCH; REPRESSED MEMORY/IMPERIAL DELETION

My husband goes to see the Patriarch in the Fener each time we're in Istanbul. I think, for him, it's like visiting a friend. The two of them are only four months apart in age.

It's astonishing that not even the successful, sophisticated manager of our hotel, with its bright lights and gold-edged ceilings, its glittering mirrors, knew where to direct us when we asked for the Fener, a real district on the Golden Horn. His face was blank, as if that time in history had been subtracted or blacked out.

GHOSTS; WINDS

Who has the time or inclination to chase after these ghosts of empire, these vapors, mere winds?

CHURCHES; MOSQUES

In a bookstore on Istiklal, I found a large selection of books on Istanbul. I picked up one that narrated a conversion of each of the city's churches into a mosque. I examined it carefully but found no words of pity or regret. I suppose that's the way it is with conquering peoples.

SIMPLICITY; HUMILITY

One craves the Patriarch's company. There's some simplicity to him and greatness in his humility that seems like a reversal of power's usual engine.

CAPITALISM: LOOT

At the airport, we ate *simit*, scattering sesame seeds, then drank Gloria Jean's coffee, carrying back simple musical instruments, nearly a hundred dollars' worth of tea and spices, sweets made of almonds, pistachios, tahini.

We had, too, that slip of paper with the carefully written addresses of the boys who'd led us to the abandoned church.

HUNGER; FIRE; APPEASEMENT; INVISIBLE

Upon arriving home, we transferred the spices from the sealed packages to jars. Now, our food will be fiery! Our mouths will burn!

Strange, all the things we put into our mouths in an effort to appease the unseen parts of ourselves.

ACKNOWLEDGMENTS

Many thanks to the editors of the publications in which the following stories first appeared:

Agni online: "Caffeine";
Blackbird: "Adam and Eva," "Until We Go to Sleep";
Chattahoochee Review: "Twenty-nine Stones for You to Hold";
Descant: "In the Time of the Girls";
Diagram: "Killing the Husband";
Dos Passos Review: "Twirling Dervishes";
The Florida Review: "Grace," "Men on Crosses";
Fourteen Hills: "Boundaries";
Front Porch Journal: "Courting Monsters";
Harpur Palate: "All the Men";
JMWW: "Being Black";
The Madison Review: "Infinity";
Our Stories: "Eros";
Prick of the Spindle: "His Mother's Cats";
Quarterly West: "Ovid Sings";
Salamander: "Anthropology," "Being Conquered";
Santa Monica Review: "Her Dowry";
Swink: "Ginka's Perfume";
Wind: "Mary";
Word Riot: "Sundering Twins".

A special thank-you to Laura LeCorgne for her consummate generosity and graceful editorial eye. Many thanks also to Martha Cooley and Bill Pierce for their fine editorial skills and support.

Thank you to students, teachers, friends, and family for hard-earned lessons. Many thanks to Jennifer Battat and Elizabeth Billings.

Infinite gratitude to Nick for ferociously protecting my desire to write, and to Constantine and Alexander for inspiration, patience, and understanding.

Loving thanks to my mother, Louise Jankelson Rosenberg, who, in her wisdom, always knew to let me be.

ABOUT THE AUTHOR

Born in San Francisco, Anne Germanacos has lived in Greece for over thirty years. Together with her husband, Nick Germanacos, she ran the Ithaka Cultural Studies Program on the islands of Kalymnos and Crete. She holds an MFA from the Bennington Writing Seminars. She and her husband have two sons.

BOA Editions, Ltd.
American Reader Series

No. 1   *Christmas at the Four Corners of the Earth*
Prose by Blaise Cendrars
Translated by Bertrand Mathieu

No. 2   *Pig Notes & Dumb Music: Prose on Poetry*
By William Heyen

No. 3   *After-Images: Autobiographical Sketches*
By W. D. Snodgrass

No. 4   *Walking Light: Memoirs and Essays on Poetry*
By Stephen Dunn

No. 5   *To Sound Like Yourself: Essays on Poetry*
By W. D. Snodgrass

No. 6   *You Alone Are Real to Me: Remembering Rainer Maria Rilke*
By Lou Andreas-Salomé

No. 7   *Breaking the Alabaster Jar: Conversations with Li-Young Lee*
Edited by Earl G. Ingersoll

No. 8   *I Carry A Hammer In My Pocket For Occasions Such As These*
By Anthony Tognazzini

No. 9   *Unlucky Lucky Days*
By Daniel Grandbois

No. 10   *Glass Grapes and Other Stories*
By Martha Ronk

No. 11   *Meat Eaters & Plant Eaters*
By Jessica Treat

No. 12   *On the Winding Stair*
By Joanna Howard

No. 13   *Cradle Book*
By Craig Morgan Teicher

No. 14   *In the Time of the Girls*
By Anne Germanacos